EVIDENCE

Evidence

IAN COLFORD

The Porcupine's Quill

Library and Archives Canada Cataloguing in Publication

Colford, Ian
    Evidence / by Ian Colford.

ISBN 978-0-88984-303-5 (pbk.)

    I. Title.

PS8555.O44E84 2008   C813´.54   C2008-900348-9

Published by The Porcupine's Quill, 68 Main St, Erin, Ontario N0B 1T0.
http://www.sentex.net/~pql

Readied for the Press by Doris Cowan.

Represented in Canada by the Literary Press Group.
Trade orders are available from University of Toronto Press.

We acknowledge the support of the Ontario Arts Council and the Canada
Council for the Arts for our publishing program. The financial support of the
Government of Canada through the Book Publishing Industry Development
Program is also gratefully acknowledged. Thanks, also, to the Government of
Ontario through the Ontario Media Development Corporation's OMDC
Book Fund.

Mary Elizabeth Colford

1920–2007

Je m'avance masqué
– Descartes

Evidence

I was teaching at a small college in a remote part of the province. The college property was surrounded by farmland and forest, but the college itself was modern and well equipped with all the latest technology. Because we were situated far from any towns or villages, everyone – all the teaching faculty and students – lived in residence on the campus.

My rooms were cramped and sparsely furnished, and because of this it was a relief to go out walking at night after I'd completed my work. After the weather grew cold I continued doing this, and on one occasion I heard the voices of some boys talking and laughing. This was not a complete surprise, even at two in the morning. The standards of the college were high and our students pushed themselves hard in order to get into the best graduate institutions, where competition was fierce. Some rowdy behaviour was inevitable and we normally tolerated minor offences such as curfew violations, and harmless pranks. But something in these voices was furtive and conniving.

They were behind one of the high-rise dormitories. I left the road and followed the concrete path that curved around to the rear of the building. A bloated silver moon hovered overhead in the clear sky. I was wearing sneakers and walked slowly and silently until I reached the back corner of the building. Here the path divided, and I took a few more careful steps on the grass until I had concealed myself behind a hedge.

In the moonlight I could see everything that was going on. A young man was on his knees facing away from me. He had been stripped to the waist and his arms were tied behind his back. Two others held him in place by the shoulders. Another young man was standing to one side with a slender stick or switch in his hand. When he turned, the moon lit up his face. It was one of my students, a boy named Kazan. I recognized him at once because in class he was always drawing attention to himself, either by asking obvious, silly questions, or ridiculing a point I was trying to make. I had complained about him to the department head, but was told that Kazan's father was a benefactor of the college and so discipline was not an option. Kazan knew this and used his teachers' powerlessness to his advantage. He spoke out of turn and with shameless disrespect, often calling us, his instructors, by our last name. Once, as dinner was being served, I heard him address the Dean this way, and though the Dean pretended not to hear him we all knew he had. I don't know why he behaved like this. One of the other teachers had told me that Kazan's parents travelled so much that the boy had basically raised himself and now felt he could do whatever he pleased. Whatever the case, Kazan was plainly challenging us, angling for a confrontation, but because his father was influential there seemed to be no solution to the problem. He was also smart; he turned in good work and completed his assignments on time, and so we could not simply give him a failing grade. Most of us had decided to put up with his impudence and hope that in the future he would not be in any of our classes.

Kazan's two accomplices pinioned the other man to the spot so he was unable to raise himself from his knees. As I watched, Kazan lifted the stick and brought it down hard. The three of them, Kazan and his two accomplices, laughed as their victim groaned with pain. I wondered why the man who was being beaten didn't cry for help, because the dormitory was right there and anyone would have heard him. Maybe it was a game, I thought. Then the kneeling man bowed his head, and this gesture of resignation told me who he was.

I knew no one when I first arrived at the college. The only people I'd had any contact with were the department head and the Dean, both of whom had interviewed me for the position I now held. However, the interviews had been conducted over the telephone, and so my knowledge of them, like their knowledge of me, had nothing personal about it. I had no idea what these two men looked like and our acquaintance did not extend beyond the formalities of the interview and the documents I'd included with my letter of application.

I had been assigned living quarters and once I'd retrieved my bags went straight there from the train station. The day was wet and grey and the campus was so isolated that I was beginning to think I'd made a serious mistake coming here. The setting was tranquil and undeniably beautiful, but after spending an hour in my room unpacking I began to miss the chaos of the city, its noise and smells and the hordes of people who were always in such a rush. The window of my fifth-floor apartment looked out over a vista of pastureland and rolling hills and green forest, and after considering the scene for a moment I felt the ache of longing for stimulation. All at once I needed to go to a Vietnamese restaurant for spicy *pho* soup. It suddenly became very important that I see a movie or attend a concert, though I'd seldom done so when I lived near cinemas and music halls. I was afraid that by coming here I had committed myself to a form of purgatory, exiled from everything I cherished, and that my brain would wither and crumble to dust before I completed my contract and escaped.

My mood had reached a low point when there was a knock on my door. I opened it on a young man with dark curly hair and a lavish smile who introduced himself as Miller. He had been on the hiring committee, knew I was arriving today, and had come to show me around. I said I was tired after my journey, but Miller would have none of it and, with kindly insistence, persuaded me to leave my room and take a tour of the campus with him.

Over the following weeks Miller and I spent a great deal of time together. He seemed to recognize that my reserved nature would not serve me well in this new setting. He forced me to attend faculty functions and to meet people. When the students arrived for the fall term and classes started, Miller arranged his schedule so we could have lunch together two or three times a week and spend an hour together most evenings. I was grateful for his company. Because the other members of my department were heavily involved in research, I rarely saw any of them outside of the library, the dining room, or the building where our offices were located.

In a short time, however, I grew uneasy and suspicious of Miller's intentions. I'd told him about the girl I'd left behind in order to take this job, but Miller did not ask anything about her and made no reference to a girlfriend of his own. In fact, whenever the subject of women came up, he spoke with surprising sharpness as he impatiently dismissed the entire sex as weak and depraved. I assumed he was joking until I realized his solitude was a natural state, that he sought it out and welcomed it. It occurred to me that apart from myself he had no friends, and I wondered how he'd spent his time before I arrived and whom I had replaced.

Soon his comments became personal. He began to flatter me, and with a knowing glance would make a remark about my hair or the shape of my nose, but introducing these as asides or with a chuckle of self-mockery, so that I could hardly tell if he was serious. Still, I began to find this constant attention cloying and tedious. To avoid him I scheduled extra tutorials with my students and assigned more papers, so that all my evenings would be occupied with marking. On weekends I made other excuses.

Finally, in the hall outside my office, he confronted me. He took my arm and, as if we'd been more than just friends, accused me of having 'found someone else'. It was ridiculous of him to speak this way, of course, and I told him so. I said that I valued our friendship, but he'd become morbidly attached to me and I would be grateful if from now on he would leave me alone. At that his mouth fell open and I thought I saw tears in his eyes. He quickly backed away and bowed his head. In the weeks that followed I still saw him almost every day. We ate our meals in the same dining hall. We attended many of the same meetings. When an encounter was unavoidable we were civil to each other. But beyond a few pleasantries we did not speak. However, his gesture of defeat remained with me.

Now, seeing the moonlit figure lower his head in that same way, I knew that Kazan's victim was my friend Miller.

I almost stepped forward to intervene, but something held me back, perhaps the crazed look in Kazan's eyes. I strained to hear what he was saying. It seemed like Kazan was asking the same question over and over again, spitting the word 'faggot' in Miller's face, and when Miller didn't answer Kazan hit him with the stick. This went on until the other two, at last growing tired of the game, dropped Miller's arms. I relaxed, thinking the assault was over. But instead of turning to leave, Kazan lifted his foot and kicked Miller in the chest. His friends were now trying to restrain him, but Kazan pushed them away and kept kicking his victim, who had fallen over backward on the ground. I was too stunned to react, and it was only after Kazan had delivered half a dozen kicks and Miller lay absolutely still that I yelled for him to stop. I threw a rock that hit one of them as they ran away. By this time, lights had come on inside the dormitory, but Kazan and his friends had disappeared.

Miller was unconscious. There was blood on his face, and marks all over his body. I cradled his head in my arms. When campus security arrived I told them what I had seen, then stood back, joining the small crowd of students that had gathered, all shivering in their night-clothes. We watched as a man with a first-aid kit attended to Miller's injuries and another spoke into a walkie-talkie requesting an ambulance. I left when I saw that Miller was receiving the help he needed.

In the morning I went to the Dean and told him what I'd witnessed and said that I was ready to put it in writing and testify in court if need be. He did not, however, seem impressed by my account and dismissed me with a wave of his hand.

'Yes,' he said. 'It's regrettable. But the matter has been resolved to the satisfaction of the college.' He managed a thin-lipped smile.

I left and tried to imagine what he meant by this. On the way to the clinic I passed through the dining hall for breakfast, and there was Kazan, with his friends, all of them filling their bellies with fried eggs and bacon. I sat down and considered my options, one of which was to take my complaint to a more senior level within the college. But before I'd finished eating I saw all three of them staring in my direction. As if he knew my thoughts, Kazan smiled and wagged his finger at me.

The clinic was located in a pretty Victorian-style house at the eastern edge of campus, a relic from earlier times. I was shown upstairs and into the room that Miller was sharing with a couple of other patients. One, an elderly man with no hair, was reading a magazine. The blinds were raised and the tall windows let in plenty of light. Gauzy curtains separated the beds. Miller seemed happy to see me, and he grasped my hand when I held it out.

'I'm so glad you've come,' he said. There were no marks on his face or arms, but it was obvious that speaking caused him discomfort.

'How are you?'

'A couple of broken ribs, but otherwise …' He paused to take a breath. 'Well, I was lucky.'

For a moment all we did was smile at each other. Casually, gently, I disengaged my hand from his.

'Kostandin, I have something to tell you,' he said at last. He lowered his eyes and feigned concern with the arrangement of the bedsheets. For a moment he fussed with them.

'What is it?'

His voice dropped to just above a whisper. 'It's kind of delicate.'

I kept quiet and looked at him as he delayed passing on his news. Finally he brought his eyes up to meet mine. The smile was gone.

'When they were beating me, they kept saying I had to tell them. They said it over and over, that I had to tell them. It was almost like they were saying it was useless for me to keep it secret, that everyone knew anyway. So I told them it was you, that we were lovers.'

All at once the room seemed intensely warm. I struggled to take a breath.

'I'm sorry,' he said. 'But I thought they were going to kill me. You understand, don't you? I had to say it. They gave me no choice.'

I backed toward the door. The elderly man scowled at me, and I realized that I had cried out in disgust. The pressure of something rising up my throat made me gag.

'I had to tell them,' Miller said.

I stumbled down the stairs and escaped outside.

S ome years before, I had been waiting tables at a restaurant and had saved enough money to pay for a week at a resort for singles. I chose this place because in the brochure it said that people travelled there from all over the world.

I had no trouble getting the time off. The couple I worked for had a pretty fourteen-year-old daughter, and because I was nice to her and sometimes helped her with her homework, her parents seemed to be worried that I, a young single man of unknown family, wanted to marry her. So when I told them where I was going and that I needed a whole week of vacation, they were glad to give it to me.

The brochure said that when my flight arrived a man would be waiting in the airport with a sign that had the name of the resort on it. When I found him and said I was with his group, he told me where to go to find the bus. There were only a few seats left when I got on. Most of the passengers were younger than me and a lot of them seemed to know each other, because everyone was talking. I heard voices speaking English, French, German, Spanish. People turned to look me over as I walked down the aisle. I saw dark- and light-skinned women, women with short hair, women with long hair, young men wearing shorts and sneakers with baseball caps reversed on their heads, girls in T-shirts who giggled when I went by. I took a seat at the back and soon we were on our way.

My companions all looked fit and tanned, like athletes. But I had already decided the girl I was looking for wouldn't be like that. She would be small and pale, with a quiet manner and a tremor in her voice. She would speak English. She would be surprised by my attention, because being neither beautiful nor rich she regarded herself as uninteresting. After working at the restaurant I was no longer interested in beauty. I served all kinds of people, and the ones who were the most difficult to please were the beautiful women. We served authentic local cuisine and our food was good, but they always found something wrong with it, or with the table setting, or the service, or their drinks. They seemed to believe that by making one complaint after another they were amusing their rich boyfriends. The more they complained the louder they laughed. It was as if the two were somehow connected.

The dusty landscape was covered with bushes and long yellow grass. The travel literature had said the island was poor, but I was not prepared for the sight of people in rags and naked children playing in the puddles left by the rains. A man with frail reed-like limbs was tilling a field, walking behind an implement hitched to a pair of emaciated oxen. Many buildings were little more than piles of rubble, and the shacks people lived in were built from salvaged stones and trash. The literature said the last war had ended more than twenty years ago, but it still looked like a battlefield. We did not pass through any towns. Soon the bus turned from the main road and took us through a set of sturdy metal gates that were shut and locked behind us. It appeared the resort was in a compound surrounded by a high wire fence. Armed guards patrolled the perimeter.

We were given rooms that fronted along an open terrace or walkway. Mine was in the south wing on the second floor. The view from the back or ocean side revealed an expanse of grass, palm trees, white sand, and water so calm and flat it was like a mirror. People strolled along stone pathways, alone, in pairs, or in groups. Nobody seemed in a hurry.

I put on my swimming trunks and went down to the bar. A young woman with red hair and an Irish accent served me a gin and tonic. I took my drink outside and sat beside the swimming pool. According to the schedule posted in my room, there was a snorkelling lesson going on down by the beach. Later someone would be teaching wind surfing. Aerobics sessions were held every couple of hours. For the non-athletes there was hula dancing and tai chi. After dinner, there was going to be a stage show in the auditorium, with magic and acrobatics. The staff of the resort would be performing. Then the disco would open and there would be music and dancing until two in the morning. Though not naturally sociable, I had decided to attend as many events as possible until I met the girl I was looking for.

That evening I had dinner with some Australians, a girl from China who was very quiet, a girl from Sweden, and a group of Americans. The Americans, all men, were the loudest ones at the table. They talked mostly about themselves, but it soon became clear they had chosen this table because of the Swedish girl. As the meal went on they asked her one question after another. She was slender and had long blond hair. She seemed to enjoy the attention, and whenever she laughed at something one of them said, the young man who had made her smile would direct a triumphant smirk at his companions. Apparently uncomfortable with the flirting, the Australians, two men and two women, talked among themselves, ate quickly, and got up to leave.

This left me with the Chinese girl. I asked her what town she was from. She nodded eagerly and said 'Yes.' I asked her another question about her home, and she nodded and again said 'Yes,' but louder than before. By this time the Americans had surrounded the Swedish girl and were telling her stories. While she laughed they took turns filling her glass with wine as fast as she could empty it. They were laughing so loudly I could hardly hear my own voice. I began to feel awkward sitting next to the Chinese girl, who glanced at me every few seconds. She seemed very sweet. I tried saying a few words to her in Spanish, German, and finally French. She spoke Chinese to me and gestured with her hands. Finally she shrugged. The frustration of not being able to communicate made us both smile, but since it was obvious we had no language in common, I excused myself and went outside to walk on the beach.

In the twilight, the distant horizon was faintly visible. The water lapped against the shore, a soft warm breeze barely disturbing the calm. A few seabirds floated overhead, riding the air. I took off my shoes and felt the sand slither between my toes. Couples walked by, holding hands. I wandered a long distance down the beach. The night was beautiful and I was reluctant to turn back. Having spent much of the day travelling, I was too tired to attend a stage show or go dancing, but I felt contented and did not want to go to bed. With the sand warming my feet and the breeze like a caress against my skin, my thoughts grew still, like an animal at rest. I had left the resort far behind when I came to the edge of the compound. The wire fence emerged from the tangle of grass and spindly bushes and cut off my progress by extending all the way across the beach and into the water. Posted on the fence was a sign that read 'No guests beyond this point.' Not far away a guard was seated on a rock, smoking a cigarette. Though the twilight had deepened into dusk, I could tell he was watching me. In his arms he cradled a machine gun.

At breakfast the next morning I saw a girl who seemed right for me. She was short and slight. Her lank brown hair had been cropped unevenly at the nape of her neck. She wore a plaid shirt over a one-piece bathing suit and the skin of her thighs was pale white except for a few red patches where she hadn't applied enough sun block. On her feet she wore pink flip-flops that slapped against her heels with each step. There was nothing remarkable about her except her eyes, which were large and deep-set beneath dark heavy brows. I followed her past the buffet as she selected her breakfast from the items on display. She took a wedge of watermelon, a chunk of pineapple, a thick slice of crusty bread, some cheese, and finally a glass of milk. I liked the way she walked, but the flip-flops slapping against her feet made her seem clumsy. As I filled a cup with coffee from the dispenser, I watched to see where she would sit. To my relief she chose one of the small tables at the edge of the dining area and sat alone.

I carried my coffee over to the table and asked if I could join her.

'Be my guest,' she said.

I introduced myself as I sat down. She didn't look at me. She was eating her watermelon using a knife and fork.

'I'm Irene,' she said. 'Some of my friends call me Sunny.'

'You're American?'

She smiled. 'Guess again.'

'British?'

'Canadian,' she said. 'Nobody remembers Canada.'

'I'm sorry.'

She laughed. 'Don't be silly. It hardly matters. Where are you from?'

'Greece.'

She tilted her head.

'But your English is so good. You must have learned that somewhere else.'

'I learned by listening to English radio broadcasts.'

'Really?'

I shrugged. 'Some people can't afford lessons.'

'Say something to me in Greek.'

'*Ti je kanadez,*' I said. '*Unë jam shqiptar. Ti je shumë bukur.*'

'That's not Greek,' she said. 'I have Greek friends. They don't talk like that.'

'It's Hungarian.'

'Oh, so you're from Hungary.'

'No.'

She smiled slowly and a pink flush appeared on her neck. 'A man of mystery. I like that.'

With her fork she pushed the stripped watermelon rind to the edge of her plate and started on the pineapple.

'Aren't you hungry? The food is really good. This fruit is incredible.'

'Coffee's enough for me.' I was taking strange delight in watching her eat, almost as if I were responsible for her well-being. 'So why do your friends call you "Sunny"?'

'Oh, they're being ironic, actually. I'm usually pretty serious. I think they're reminding me that there's more to life than endangered species and child labour and capital punishment. Some things are just for fun.'

'Like this resort.'

She nodded.

'Are you here alone?'

'My friend Sylvia was supposed to come. But she cancelled after she read stuff about the island, about the poverty and how corrupt the government is. Did you know there are children in this country dying from diseases that have been wiped out everywhere else on earth? We're eating like kings and queens when people here can't grow enough to keep themselves going because everything is so run down. The government takes kickbacks from places like this, but all they do is build themselves bigger houses. None of the money goes to the people who need it.'

'And yet you're here,' I said, 'having a good time.'

'Having a wonderful time,' she said, laughing.

'When did you arrive?'

'Last night. Did you see all the guards around the gate? Isn't it enough to freak you out?'

I nodded. 'What are your plans for the day?'

She took a drink of milk.

'Snorkelling in a few minutes. That's the morning gone. Then I'll come back and have lunch and take a rest. I might go for a walk in the afternoon, or maybe just lounge on the beach. I like the way everything's so flexible. You can do everything or nothing. What are you going to do?'

'Today I think I'll just go swimming. But I'll check the schedule first to see if anything looks interesting.'

She nodded.

'Do you mind if I ask if we can have dinner together? Not alone together,' I added quickly when a look of panic flashed across her face. 'But just meet ahead of time and sit at the same table. You're the first person I've spoken to. I was with some Americans last night and I didn't get to do much talking.'

'God, Americans!' She rolled her eyes. 'Aren't they incredible?' She nodded. 'Dinner with a familiar face would be nice. We can continue our conversation. Maybe I'll find out where you're really from.'

I suggested I knock on her door at an appointed time. She was in room 311. We agreed on seven that evening.

She glanced at her watch and stood.

'I have to go. The boat leaves at nine. They're taking us to a deep bay where there's lots of underwater stuff to see.'

I stood as well.

'I'll see you tonight.'

She smiled and held out her hand. It felt cool and very small in mine.

'I'll be there,' she said.

I watched her go. There was something endearingly innocent about her choice of footwear; something intimate and alluring as well – as if she'd just stepped out of the shower and into my company. I sat and finished my coffee. I was glad that I'd asked about dinner. She seemed like someone I could spend time with and whose company wouldn't become tiresome. And her manner was open and natural. I could ask her anything and without thinking twice she'd tell me the truth.

The rest of the morning I amused myself on the beach. The water was warm and formed a perfectly straight line against the horizon. A few wispy clouds floated high above. There were a lot of beautiful women walking back and forth wearing skimpy bikinis. I thought about Irene and wondered how she was doing with her snorkelling lesson. I was looking forward to dinner because we would have a lot to talk about. I wanted to know all about her life in Canada, what she did for a living, where she had grown up, what her passions were. If our personalities and interests meshed the way I hoped, at the end of the week I would ask her for her address and telephone number so we could correspond. Then at some point I would travel to Canada and visit her.

Just before lunch I saw a large motorboat round the cape to the south of the beach. I gathered my things and followed its approach into the resort's marina. From a distance I recognized a couple of the resort staff, a man at the wheel and a woman holding a rope. The others in the boat were guests. Irene sat among them in her black one-piece bathing suit chatting with a girl in a bikini. I watched until the boat was tethered to the pier and the guests began to disembark. Then I returned to my room to take a shower.

For much of the afternoon I stayed by the pool. It was very hot beneath an intense sun, and soon I had joined some others in the shade of the covered bar. Eventually I went back to my room and fell asleep. When I awoke I was worried that I had slept into the dinner hour, but according to the clock there was still plenty of time before I was to meet Irene. I took another shower and dressed in a loose-fitting linen suit. When I was ready I went upstairs to find room 311.

I knocked on her door and waited. After a minute I knocked again. I thought maybe she had slipped out for a moment or two, so I leaned against the railing to wait. After five minutes, a group passed by. Among them I recognized the Americans from the previous night. We all smiled and greeted each other cordially. When they had gone down the stairs I knocked on Irene's door again, in case she had been in the shower. There was still no answer. Then it occurred to me that despite our arrangement she might be waiting for me by the dining area. I went down and looked, but she wasn't there. I went over to the bar. She wasn't by the pool either. I returned to her room and knocked on the door again. I called her name, hoping to wake her if she had fallen asleep, but there was no answer. Again I leaned against the railing. After several minutes the door next to hers opened and a young woman in a blue T-shirt, harem pants and black oriental-style slippers emerged. I asked if she knew the girl in 311 but she said no. When she was gone I lit a cigarette. Other people went by, talking and laughing, but I didn't speak to any of them. At eight o'clock I gave up and returned downstairs.

The thought passed through my mind that she was forgetful and had joined another group for dinner, perhaps her snorkelling companions from that morning. But I didn't see her anywhere in the dining room. Then I thought maybe she'd regretted our arrangement and was staying in her room to avoid me. If this was the case, she might have brought food with her so she wouldn't have to go out at all.

I carried my plate from the buffet into the dining area and took the last seat at a table for eight. On the way I saw the Chinese girl at another table. I greeted her, but she was speaking with some other Chinese people and didn't look at me. My dinner companions were again from around the globe. We chatted and laughed, but I missed Irene's unpretentious charm and wished she was there. After the meal was over I followed a few of the others out to the bar, where we ordered drinks. There was to be another stage presentation tonight, this time showcasing the talent of some of the guests. There would be singing, dancing and acrobatics. We talked about this and other things as we sat by the pool with our drinks.

Irene was not at breakfast the next morning. After eating I went up to her room and knocked on the door, but there was no answer. I was beginning to think she'd been taken ill, but since I couldn't be sure of this I didn't know how to proceed. It was also possible she'd been contacted about a family emergency and had left the resort. Since it was none of my business and there was nothing I could do, I went back to my room and made my preparations to go swimming. When I got to the beach, I spread my towel on the lounge chair and stretched out beneath the morning sun.

After only twenty minutes I left and returned to my room. There was nobody around. All the guests were out enjoying the day's activities. I went upstairs and stood outside the door of room 311 to see if there was a way to break in. I twisted the knob and pressed, but the door held fast. I was still standing there a few minutes later when a woman pushing a cart laden with cleaning supplies and fresh towels came around the corner. She unlocked the door of another room and carried a stack of towels and linens inside.

I went down to the other end of the terrace and interrupted her. I said I'd left my key at the beach and needed to get into my room. She followed me out and along the terrace, moving slowly on her thick legs.

'Weech won your room, boy? Weech won?'

I indicated the door numbered 311.

'Thees your room, boy?'

She sorted through the keys on her ring and used one to unlock the door.

'Thank you,' I said, but she had walked away.

This room resembled my own in every respect, including the sparse bamboo furnishings and walls painted a peachy orange. Even the watercolour print above the desk, which depicted an island street scene, was the same.

A suitcase lay open on the bed, which had either been re-made this morning or not slept in. The suitcase held a colourful assortment of neatly folded summer clothing. On the floor beside the bed was a smaller shoulder bag. This was open as well and contained mostly undergarments along with a small cosmetics bag and some bath supplies. A tan-coloured linen jacket had been draped over the back of a chair.

In the bathroom the shower stall was dry. The towels had been disturbed but these were dry now as well.

I examined the suitcase again. Attached to the handle was a tag that read, 'Irene Hatcher,' followed by an address in Canada.

There was nothing I could do here. I closed the door behind me when I left.

Because of the size of the resort there was a chance that our paths had simply not crossed since that morning at breakfast, that she had, after all, managed to avoid me. I went downstairs to the main office and asked the receptionist at the desk if I could leave a message for my friend in room 311. She gave me a card and an envelope and told me to write out the message and seal it inside. I wrote that I needed urgently to speak with her, signed my name, and added my room number. On the outside of the envelope I wrote, 'Irene Hatcher,' and handed it over. The girl said the envelope would be kept in the office and that they would notify Miss Hatcher that a message was waiting for her. When I asked how this would be done, since the rooms had no telephones, she explained that she would go up now and tape a notice to the door of room 311 asking Irene to come to the main office to pick up an envelope.

I thanked her and went back to my room. After waiting half an hour I went upstairs to check, and, as the girl had said, there was a note taped to the door of room 311 informing Miss Hatcher that an envelope was waiting for her in the main office.

I had done everything I could. That afternoon I returned to the beach.

Over the days that followed I took part in some group excursions, signed up for classes in windsurfing and scuba diving, and spent a lot of time sunbathing. I ate each meal with a different group and though I always looked for Irene in the dining room, I never saw her. I tried to put her out of my mind and kept away from her room. However curiosity got the better of me. After only two days I went upstairs again to find the note still taped to the door. The following morning I checked at the office and was told that Miss Hatcher had not picked up her message.

I enjoyed my week at the resort, but other than Irene I did not meet any girls I wanted to keep in touch with. On the morning of the day I was to fly home I went for a final walk along the beach. The weather had turned cloudy. A wind had come up from the south, and it was sultry rather than warm. The surf rolled rhythmically across the sand, depositing debris and seaweed on the shore. I smelled the salt and felt it on my skin and in my hair. I walked slowly, as if this would delay my leaving. The wind carried masses of clouds across the sky, piling them up until they loomed, grey and threatening. The swirling sea had turned the colour of pewter. Finally the first drops of rain hit my face and pitted the sand. But it was a gentle rain that left me invigorated.

I had walked almost as far as I had on the first day. I was approaching the fence, where the sign would tell me I could go no further. The guard was not at his post. Again I turned to look at the water. A cruise ship sat on the horizon, apparently motionless. The water churned and whitecaps rolled in the distance. Then my attention was drawn to an object bobbing in a pool of water between some rocks. It was tossed upward by the movement of a wave and drawn back into the shallows. I waded into the sea to investigate. But it was only a piece of pink foam plastic that had drifted to shore.

The airport bus had arrived, but before getting on I went upstairs to room 311. The door was open. A policeman wearing rubber gloves was picking through the contents of Irene's suitcase, lifting out each garment and examining it before setting it aside. He paused when he saw me in the doorway and looked at me intently for what seemed like a long time. Neither of us spoke. Then he returned to his work and I went downstairs and got on the bus.

I noticed the boy in the wheelchair before I noticed his mother. Even from a distance, as they crossed the hot dusty square in front of the hotel, there was something physically odd about him, something disproportionate and unsettling. His head was too large for his body, and his forehead protruded, casting a shadow over the rest of his face. He was chewing, or perhaps talking; his mouth opened and closed with a sort of mechanical regularity. His mother pushed the wheelchair, followed by two of the local boys carrying their bags.

She was Mrs Lamond. Her son's name was Stefan. Though it was late in the day when they arrived, they were expected, and I was given the task of carrying their bags up to their room, which was on the fifth floor. It was an old building with narrow hallways crammed with antiques, and the wheelchair was wide and bulky. Although it had a motor and the right armrest was fitted with a little box with buttons and switches, Mrs Lamond insisted on pushing the contraption, her son apparently disinclined or unable to control the chair himself. Mrs Kent, the English lady who ran the hotel, showed Stefan and his mother into the lift, but because there was not enough room for her to follow after them, they went up by themselves. It took me two trips to carry all of their bags up the five flights of narrow, winding stairs.

These events took place while I was living on Spetsos Island. I had been there for a few months and was slowly picking up the language, but it was a difficult process. Before arriving in Greece I had known only my own country, where adults are soft-spoken and children play quiet, solitary games. I didn't understand the locals, whose every conversation consisted of bickering and yelling and wild gesticulations. I was still trying to get used to brawls and shouting matches that turned out to be discussions of the weather. I hadn't made any friends. Shortly after I came here I was cornered by a group of local boys about my age, around sixteen, who held me down and made me eat a cigarette butt, so I spent my free time alone, trying to avoid trouble.

That evening, after Mrs Lamond arrived, I was waiting at the port, which was crowded because a ferry was expected. I carried a sign with the name of our hotel written on it, and held it up after the ferry docked and the passengers began crowding out of the terminal. I was accustomed to rough treatment at the hands of rivals from other hotels in the area. A bit of jostling was normal as we all tried to get the attention of these new visitors to the island. Today, however, the competition was fiercer than usual, and as we jockeyed for position the sign was knocked out of my hand and fell to the ground. I tried to get it back, but someone was standing on it and wouldn't move. In the scuffle that followed, I was turned around and pushed toward the street, where I stumbled and fell. I got up and ran back into the crowd, but I no longer had a sign to hold up to identify myself with a hotel. Anyone I approached would think I was a con-artist or a beggar, and probably call the police. I thrust my hands into my pockets and wandered away from the noise of the port, dodging cars and motorcycles as I went until, from a safe distance, I turned and looked back. The hotel employees who had pushed me down were escorting their new customers away. I was still angry, but since I couldn't do anything about it I decided to go back to Mrs Kent's hotel. I had a room to myself behind the kitchen, where I slept on a cot. I had just come within sight of the hotel when I saw Mrs Lamond and Stefan emerge from the front door.

She easily manoeuvred the wheelchair down the single step to street level and turned away from the port toward the town's business district. Out of curiosity I followed, keeping a distance of about twenty paces behind them. I noticed she had changed her clothes. When I first saw her she had been wearing flat shoes, a loose-fitting cotton dress, and a straw hat with a wide brim. Tonight she wore a dress of a darker material cinched in at the waist, shoes with high heels, and a kerchief tied elaborately into her hair, which – let down – was nearly shoulder length. I had not taken particular notice of her face or physical bearing earlier, and I now found myself trying to calculate her age, and that of her son. Unconsciously I suppose, I had guessed her to be about the same age as Mrs Kent, who had greying hair and fussy mannerisms and seemed very old. But now, as Mrs Lamond propelled her son along the street, she struck me as a much younger woman, perhaps in her early thirties. I had to step smartly to keep up with her.

She turned a corner and proceeded along one of the narrow passageways leading away from the harbour. I'd assumed she was a stranger here, but she seemed to know where she was going. Moving quickly now she turned again, but when I reached the corner she was nowhere in sight. However, the wheelchair made a clatter as she pushed it over the cobblestones, and I was able to catch up in time to see her stop outside a small building with a sign suspended above the door.

It was that moment with no definition when dusk gives way to night. The evening light was failing and the buildings all around us were in shadow. I couldn't see her face as she took the metal knocker in her hand and rapped loudly on the door. Stefan sat quietly by her side. Just as the door opened a light came on, and an elderly gentleman in a white smock came out on the step and greeted her with a polite smile and a handshake. I couldn't hear what they were saying, and I still couldn't read the sign, which was in the local language and for me indecipherable. The man bent down and said something to Stefan, taking the boy's limp hand in his and holding it for a moment. He and Mrs Lamond lifted the wheelchair over the step and through the narrow entranceway. In a few seconds the door was closed and the light switched off. Since I was tired and not feeling adventurous, I returned to the hotel and went to bed.

At this time of year arrivals and departures were routine. I took little notice of the guests and their comings and goings, and quickly forgot them the minute they were gone. Even while they were with us I found it very difficult to remember names and faces. In any case, my interaction with them was limited to carrying bags and cleaning rooms, and most were absent while I went about my daytime errands.

Occasionally, when the other chores were done, Mrs Kent allowed me to serve tea in the drawing room. If the weather was poor we might have as many as twenty people, seated and standing, drinking the orange pekoe tea and eating the imported cakes and biscuits of which Mrs Kent was so fond and which, as she said – always with a dramatic sigh – were a reminder that she was a foreigner and far far away from her native England. Normally, however, since most people visited the island because of the sultry Aegean climate and wanted to spend their days lounging on the beach or trekking through the mountains of the interior, the parlour was empty but for us and two or three elderly or sunburned guests.

Today, as four o'clock approached, it appeared that Mrs Kent and I would be spending the tea hour alone, passing each other biscuits and making inconsequential conversation. I was preparing to set out the tray with two cups and saucers when I heard the familiar muted roar of the lift as it made its descent. When I entered the drawing room Mrs Kent was greeting Stefan and Mrs Lamond and inviting the latter to take a seat.

Once our guests were settled Mrs Kent moved about the room without evident purpose. I placed the tray on the sideboard. My employer was a friendly woman who thrived on idle conversation, routine, and the regularity of habit. She loved her guests and could waste entire mornings chatting with them in the breakfast room. She had come here, she told me, many years ago, with her husband. The hotel was to provide them with an income for their retirement. The business was so demanding that her husband, who was older than she, wearied of it within a couple of years, and returned to England. Mrs Kent had grown fond of her new home and decided to stay, as she put it, 'for a few more months' before selling. Those few months had turned into years. But somehow she had never gotten used to the nature of the business, which could throw surprises at you faster than you could catch them. She admitted to me once, over tea, that maybe she was not suited to operating this kind of establishment. And it was true: anything unexpected or unusual could send her skittering about the house waving her arms, scolding the help and annoying the guests. The best we could hope for at such times was that she would go out shopping and leave it to her employees to cope with the problem. Today, I could see that the presence of Stefan in the drawing room was making her very nervous. She drifted to the far end of the room and would not look at our guests.

I approached Mrs Lamond. 'Will your son be having tea?'

I expected her to say no.

'Yes, please. Thank you very much.'

I returned to the sideboard and poured a cup for each of them. When I gave Mrs Lamond her cup she thanked me, placed it on the table in front of her, and reached for the pitcher of milk. This left me with Stefan's cup. It was plain he could not hold it himself, much less drink from it.

'Here is fine,' Mrs Lamond said, indicating the table.

I set the cup down.

'I like to include him as much as possible.' She sipped her tea, made a face, and added more milk.

Mrs Kent had by this time recovered her composure and was at the sideboard pouring tea for herself. I went to the kitchen for the tray of biscuits. When I brought them out, Mrs Kent had taken the seat next to Mrs Lamond, a position that saved her from having to interact in any way with Stefan, or even for that matter acknowledge his existence.

I presented the tray.

'You have a lovely hotel,' Mrs Lamond commented as she selected a biscuit for herself and then some for Stefan, which she balanced on the rim of his saucer.

'Thank you.'

'You've been here for quite some time, I gather?'

'Fourteen years.'

Mrs Kent then launched into her favourite story, of how she had come to be the proprietor of a hotel on a beautiful, paradisal island thousands of miles from her home. While she talked, I sat down opposite them and observed Stefan, something I had not had a chance to do until this moment. His deformity was disconcerting, and his eyes seemed to stare all around without taking anything in. As well, he moved incessantly. He nodded, grimaced, waved his arms and kicked his legs, but there was in all these movements a restrained and gentle quality, as if he were determined that his condition cause as little disruption as possible for those around him. He also seemed perfectly content, in the manner of a happy infant.

'He was born this way,' Mrs Lamond said.

'I'm sorry?' I had been so wrapped up in my contemplation of the boy that I had not noticed the turn in the conversation.

'Poor Stefan,' she said. She was watching me. 'He's been like this all his life.'

I placed my cup and saucer on the table.

'I must apologize –' Mrs Kent began.

I realized then that I had been staring at him in a manner that must have appeared quite rude. I didn't know what to say.

Mrs Lamond dismissed our concerns with a wave of her hand.

'It takes some getting used to. It's not what one expects. And I'm afraid I was not altogether forthcoming when I contacted you and asked that you save us a room. After you said it was on the top floor, it was enough that I knew you had a lift. But I could have said something about the wheelchair and the disabilities. It's just that I get so tired of explaining the same thing over and over that sometimes I can't bring myself to talk about it.'

There was a silence.

'Can he hear us or understand what we're talking about?' I asked.

'There's some uncertainty about what he can and cannot understand. As you might imagine, I've consulted a lot of doctors, but they all have different opinions. They're in agreement that his grasp of language is probably less than that of a ten-month-old baby, which is to say he'll respond to my voice but the words themselves are immaterial. I've travelled up and down Europe trying to find out if anything can be done. I'm not looking for a cure, but I would like to know if he's capable of learning anything at all, or if he will ever enjoy music, or the sound of birds singing, or the wind on his face. It would be nice for me to know if he understands who I am. But I'm afraid I'm not much farther along now than I was when I started. Being the way he is, he can't reveal anything about his world, and so it's all guesswork on the part of the doctors. I'm sensitive to his needs because of my mother's intuition, but even that only takes you so far. I can't see the world through his eyes, and I'll never know what it's like to sit in that chair.'

Stefan waved his hands and seemed to look around the room in fascination. The way he paddled his arms and flexed his legs made me think of someone immersed in water. It was as if he were still negotiating the amniotic fluid of his mother's womb.

'How old is he?' I asked.

'Fifteen,' Mrs Lamond said. She reached across and brushed Stefan's hair where it had strayed over his forehead. 'He's a riddle I've been trying to solve for fifteen years.'

There was a pause in the conversation while Mrs Kent refilled our cups and we all took more milk and sugar. Then we discussed the weather, the discomforts of making the journey from Athens by ferry, the recent currency crisis. Presently a few of the other guests returned from their day at the beach and it was time to put the tea things away. I said I could help Mrs Lamond take Stefan up to their room.

'Well, thank you,' she said, surprising me again, because I had fully expected her to say she could manage on her own.

I pushed Stefan's chair for the first time, through the doorway of the drawing room and into the hall. This was not simple because the hall was narrow and cluttered. Trying not to jolt Stefan, I backed into the lift and shifted the chair to one side to make a space for Mrs Lamond. There was just enough room for the three of us. I looked at her face as we rode up. Her features were delicate and her skin had a healthy sheen, but below the surface was the pallor of a recent illness. She was a handsome woman, but I was more curious than attracted. She turned toward me and our eyes met. Neither of us looked away. I went on studying her, and as I did so, she seemed to study me.

We did not speak on the way up, and when the doors opened I pushed the chair out. Mrs Lamond silently led the way to their room and unlocked the door. I pushed the chair across the threshold. I checked that Stefan was all right and then looked at her. She stood with her hands folded, staring into a corner of the room and holding her head tilted slightly downward. She seemed to be collecting her strength, and I felt I was being given a glimpse of her private self, the one who dealt with Stefan on a moment-by-moment basis. What must it be like, I wondered, to spend all your days living with someone who depended on you for everything?

All I could think of to say was, 'I can take care of him. If you want to go out.'

She raised her head and smiled. 'That's so nice of you. But we'll be fine.'

'If you show me,' I said.

But she gestured to indicate that I should leave. At her approach I backed into the hallway. I didn't take my eyes from her as she closed the door.

The next evening I ate early and was waiting in the drawing room when she brought Stefan down in the lift. She paused in the hallway when she saw me, but only for an instant before heading toward the front entrance. I opened the door and she let me roll the chair off the step and into the street. I was feeling more comfortable pushing the chair. It took almost no effort at all.

'I can help you,' I said, once we had started on our way. I assumed she was paying another visit to the old gentleman in the smock.

She was silent for a moment and then said, 'I know you can.'

'So, will you let me?'

I was encouraged when she didn't respond immediately. For a few moments I could pretend that she was considering my offer.

'I don't understand you,' she said finally, after we had gone a distance. 'Stefan and I are only here for a visit. We're leaving in a day or two. I really can't do anything for you.'

'You might come back.'

She shook her head. 'I'm only here to talk to a doctor. He's a famous neurologist. He's worked wonders with children like Stefan.'

'He lives up here, doesn't he?' I asked as we turned a corner.

When she looked at me I added, 'Last night I followed you.'

We went along in silence. The only sound was the clatter of the chair wheels as they rolled over the cobblestones. I noticed that she was falling behind and that she'd bowed her head as if deep in thought. I turned the last corner. Up ahead I saw the building with the sign suspended above the door. When she reached out and grasped my arm I stopped and held the chair still.

'What do you want?'

She looked into my eyes with the same quality of forceful innocence that had impressed me earlier. Less than forty-eight hours ago I had mistaken her for a mature woman of middle age, but tonight I could imagine her to be much younger, young enough for us to be lovers. Her skin bore not a single blemish. Her nose was small and delicate. Her strong jaw was set in an attitude of defiance, but there was moisture in her eyes. We were so close I could have cupped her cheek in my hand and stroked her neck. But her gaze narrowed as she watched me. She was suspicious because I had not yet proven that I could be trusted.

'I want you to take me with you.'

She laughed. 'That's absurd.' Then, softening her tone, 'What would either of us gain from that?'

I said that if she took me with her, I would look after Stefan for as long as she liked. I would do everything for him and she wouldn't have to pay me as long as I was given food and a place to sleep. I could get a travel permit from the consulate in Athens. It would only take a few days. Once she had no further need of me I would find other work and be out of her life.

She let go of my arm and resumed walking in the direction of the doctor's building. I followed with Stefan.

'Admit it,' I said. 'You enjoy having someone to push Stefan's chair.'

She took the knocker and rapped it loudly against the door. She looked at me.

'Be here when we're finished. It shouldn't take any longer than two hours.'

I moved out of the way so she could take the handgrips, then stepped back so that I was standing in shadow when the doctor opened the door and greeted her and Stefan.

I lit a cigarette and sat on the front step of a darkened house just down the street. The night air was sultry from the day's heat. I was close enough to the doctor's house to see her immediately when she came out.

I tried not to let my hopes rise too far. After all, nothing was certain. No promises had been made. I drew on the cigarette and focused on the doctor's house. The windows were lit, but there were no signs of people moving around.

I could see something was wrong the moment Mrs Lamond and Stefan emerged from the house. I looked at my watch. They had only been inside for twenty minutes. The doctor stood in the doorway watching as she hurriedly pushed Stefan's chair off the step and away from the house. He gazed after her for a moment, then shut the door.

She shook her head when I asked what had happened, but she let me push the chair and she walked by my side as we turned toward the harbour and the hotel.

We were both silent until we reached the street that ran along the waterfront. Mrs Lamond put her hand on my arm. 'Let's go over here,' she said, indicating a row of benches beneath some trees closer to the water.

We crossed the street. There was no ferry expected and so the evening was quiet and there was little traffic. A couple of stray dogs trotted behind us, sniffing each other. One was black with pointed ears and the other had longer hair, which was brown and dirty. They were so thin I could count their ribs. From the side closest to the water I could look down the full length of the street, which was lined with restaurants and hotels similar to Mrs Kent's all the way to the ferry terminal, after which the street curved out of sight. Beyond the town were hills that rose to become mountainous in the island's interior. I had never witnessed the view from the island's highest point.

The locals claimed that on a clear day you could see for more than a hundred miles in any direction.

The dogs wandered away as I moved Stefan into place beside the bench. I sat next to him and Mrs Lamond sat next to me. Stefan made a gurgling sound that drew my attention. His mother remained stiffly still. I reached out and took the boy's hand in mine. It was soft and limp, but warm, like a small animal that had just that moment died. When I squeezed there was no response, no indication that by touching his hand I had made any impression on him. He turned his head from side to side and his mouth opened and closed as if he were chewing. His uncomprehending eyes stared out to sea, where the sun was sinking toward the horizon.

'I appreciate your interest,' Mrs Lamond said after a few moments. 'But I'm not sure I can offer you anything. You're going to have to give me time to think.'

I nodded.

She remained silent for a minute or two, during which the sound of the surf washing over the rocks drowned out everything else.

'The doctor said there's nothing to be done. Stefan will remain the way he is for the rest of his life. But he found a problem. It's not unusual, he said, for children like Stefan to suffer a build-up of fluid in the skull. He said that I should take Stefan to a specialist right away to have a shunt put in. This won't solve the problem, however, and he said that I should prepare myself for it to get progressively worse. He said that children like Stefan usually die before they reach the age of twenty, but before they die they suffer horribly because the build-up of fluid on the brain causes pressure. This can go on for months. He can see from his test results that it's already beginning to happen.'

I murmured that I was sorry, but beyond this I wasn't sure how to react. Was she saying she did not need me, or that she needed me all the more? I could still be of use to her. Bedridden or not, I could take care of him until he died.

I kept holding his hand, even though I was beginning to find its soft clammy warmth repulsive.

'I don't want him to suffer.' She leaned over and covered her face.

'Oh, God. I should have seen this coming. I've been so selfish.'

I released Stefan's hand. As she wept, Mrs Lamond's body shuddered.

In a minute she pulled herself upright and wiped her nose on the back of her sleeve. 'It looks like I have some decisions to make.' She stood and straightened her skirt. I was pleased that she could cry in front of me and not be embarrassed.

I took my place behind Stefan's chair and we started back toward the hotel.

'I don't want you to take too much encouragement from what I'm about to say, because I haven't made up my mind yet what to do, but your kindness toward us has affected me deeply.'

I looked at her but kept my mouth shut. I didn't want to risk saying the wrong thing.

'An illness like Stefan's isolates you. I don't really have any friends. I spend all my time with him. It's not healthy, but until you made your offer I didn't see that I had any choice. I'm not rich, but I suppose we've lived in relative comfort up to now. If this doctor is right, I'll be spending more on care in the near future. Having someone with me would ease the burden. I'm tired of being alone.'

We walked the rest of the way in silence. Together we lifted Stefan's chair over the front step of the hotel and pushed it through the door. I entered the lift with her as if I were expected to do so, as if it were my duty. Our eyes locked as the lift made its slow and fretful ascent to the fifth floor. What was she thinking? What kind of impression had I made? I wanted so badly to touch her. I even moved my arm, thinking I might, but then didn't. When the door opened I pushed the chair out and followed her down the hall to their room. She unlocked the door and went inside. I pushed Stefan's chair across the threshold and then turned and left, closing the door behind me.

I found it hard to sleep that night, and the next morning when I got up it was still dark. My mind was racing, and despite an effort to keep my hopes in check, my head was filled with visions of London and New York conjured from pictures I had seen in books and newspapers. My morning tasks, mopping the floors, setting the tables in the dining room, were at least a distraction.

At that hour the hotel seemed deserted, but I heard snores and groans as I crept up the stairs and along the hall to Mrs Lamond's room. I stood outside the door and listened. There were no sounds, and for a moment I was certain that she and Stefan had left during the night and were at this moment on a ferry bound for Athens. However, one of the advantages of living on an island is that it's easy to keep track of arrivals and departures, and I knew that the next ferry would not reach port until eleven that morning.

I did not see her until after we had started serving breakfast. I was carrying a tray of soiled dishes and cutlery back to the kitchen. I rounded a corner and suddenly she stood before me. She was dressed to go out. The morning was already hot and she wore the light cotton dress and flat shoes I had seen her wearing on the first day. Earlier there had been an order for breakfast from her room, but I had not been the one to take it up. It occurred to me that I had not seen Stefan eat a single thing during their time here and that every morsel that entered his mouth would first pass through her hands.

'You must do something for me,' she said, gripping my arm and almost making me drop the tray. She actually glanced over her shoulder, as if afraid that someone might be close enough to hear.

'Yes,' I replied. My throat had dried up at the sight of her. 'Anything.'

'Stay with Stefan while I go out. There are some things I have to do and it will be much quicker if I do them alone.'

'Is he upstairs now?'

She pressed the room key into my free hand.

'He's up and dressed and in his chair. All you have to do is watch him.'

As I looked into her eyes she tightened her grip on my arm. The terrible urgency in her actions made the breath catch in my throat.

'Is something the matter?'

'No, of course not. I just don't like him to be alone for very long. Can you do this or should I ask someone else?'

I went to the kitchen and left the tray on the counter beside the sink. I would have to wash them later, but I would explain to Mrs Kent that I had been called away to perform a courtesy for a guest.

She was waiting for me in the hallway, beside the lift. The door was already open.

'You must get used to being with him,' she said. She took my hand briefly and then let it go as I entered the lift. She kept looking at me as the door slid shut.

I got out on the fifth floor and used the key to enter her room. As she had said, Stefan was in his chair. She had positioned him at the window, which offered a view of the town from the rear of the hotel. I went over and looked out of the window and then down at him. He showed no sign that he knew I was standing beside him. He moved his head about and opened and closed his mouth with the same mechanical rhythm as always. I left him for a moment to wash my hands. In the bathroom there were some toiletries lined up on the shelf beneath the mirror. I returned to the other room and sat down where I could keep Stefan in view. The room had been tidied. Bright morning light streamed in through the window.

The thought of leaving the island did not cause me any regrets. It was a temporary refuge, a station along the way. I had known the moment I arrived here that my journey would continue, and so I had purposely built no friendships. Even Mrs Kent, though she treated me with kindness, was only an employer who would find someone to fill my place the moment it became vacant. The locals were barbarians. I would not mourn the loss of their company.

As soon as we arrived in Athens I would have to go to the consulate and begin filling out forms and making sure my papers were in order. No doubt I would have to pay bribes or else they would keep me waiting for weeks while my request languished on somebody's desk. This was the way my people conducted their business, and I didn't mind paying. I only hoped that I had saved enough money to keep the delays to a minimum. I did not want Mrs Lamond to become discouraged and decide to leave me behind after all.

Stefan made a noise as if he were clearing his throat. I had been around him long enough to know it meant nothing. For a moment I thought I could hear someone moving in the corridor. I had been busy since very early that morning and as I sat in the hot airless room waiting for Mrs Lamond to return, my attention flagged and I was overcome by drowsiness. In an effort to remain conscious I sat up straight and shifted repeatedly in the chair. I wiped the sweat off my brow and shook my head, but I was tired from the excitement of the previous days and the room was stuffy, and I simply could not stay awake. Soon I had drifted into an agitated, uncomfortable sleep.

But I couldn't rest because I was aware that Mrs Lamond would not be pleased to see me asleep on the job. In my dreams she stormed into the room and scolded me for my lack of responsibility before banishing me from her presence. In one sequence she slapped my face in order to wake me. Over and over I suffered the shame of exposure, pleaded with her to give me another chance, and finally accepted the harshness of her verdict. Over and over I felt the panicked throbbing of my heart and the heat of blood rushing to my face.

Far off in the distance of my dream landscape I heard the pro-longed low-pitched blast of the ferry signalling that it was pulling out of the harbour. In an instant I was on my feet. It was now after eleven o'clock, more than two hours since she had approached me down-stairs in the hallway. Stefan had not moved from beside the window. The room suddenly seemed too tidy. I began a search. Beneath the bed I found one suitcase. The only clothes in the wardrobe belonged to Stefan. In the bathroom there was a single toothbrush, one bar of soap. I recalled how she had steered me toward the lift, drawing my attention away from the fact that she was wearing her travelling clothes by taking my hand into hers. I looked at Stefan seated in his chair, uncomprehending. I approached him, knelt by his side, and took his hand. In it was a crumpled piece of paper. I unfolded it and read, 'Forgive me.'

The plane went down at night in a thunderstorm, almost a mile short of a rural landing strip somewhere in Northern India. Everyone was killed. I heard the report on the radio the next morning while I was eating breakfast. The news did not make much of an impression on me. I forgot about it as soon as the newscast ended. It was only when I arrived on campus that I learned that one of our students, along with her entire family, had been on the plane.

The dead girl's name was Anitra Siddiqui. She was a second-year student who had planned to go into nursing. At our small college, most people either knew or knew of one another, and for the whole day the news of her death was the only topic of discussion. I tried to conduct my classes as usual, but the students were clearly preoccupied, their thoughts with their dead classmate. Nobody would look at me or answer the questions I posed, so after a while I gave up and asked if anyone wanted to say a few words about the girl who had been killed. Several people raised their hands and stood to speak. A couple of girls wept quietly, using their fingers to wipe away the tears.

Anitra Siddiqui had not been a student of mine. Later, when I saw her picture, I could not remember ever having seen her before. But like everybody else, I was consumed with morbid curiosity, and I read all the articles about her family that appeared in the newspapers. The details continued to fascinate me, even after I'd read them many times in different reports. Her father was a surgeon, her mother a laboratory technician. Her brother attended a local university and had been taking computer science. By all accounts they were hard-working, ambitious, civic-minded, and temperate in their habits. They had travelled to India because the father's remaining relatives were elderly and if he had not taken his children to visit them now, they would probably never meet at all. He had left home many years before, and though he made several return visits alone, this was the first time he had been able to take his family with him. The last leg of their journey was to carry them into a steppe region, high in the mountains of the Punjab. But without warning the weather turned severe, and they had to delay their flight for twenty-four hours. Finally they boarded the plane, a small twin-engine commuter aircraft built in Russia thirty years ago. There were fifteen passengers and a single crew member. The flight was to last forty-five minutes. The article said that the weather was clear when they took off, but there were high winds in the area where they were headed. Then, unexpectedly, clouds moved in. It was a very dark night, with no moon. The plane must have lost power because as they neared their destination radio contact became sporadic, and a few minutes before the crash the pilot reported that he was flying without the aid of instruments. He didn't have enough fuel to go back. Just as the plane was approaching the landing strip it started to rain. He was on course, and would have made it if he had maintained altitude, but from the crash pattern it appeared he'd either mistaken a field for a runway or decided to ditch the plane. The ground was soft and uneven. Upon impact the plane flipped over and broke into pieces. The people died of trauma, either from being thrown great distances outside the plane, or tossed violently about inside.

The girl smiling at me from the newspaper page was pretty, and I detected keen intelligence in her eyes. The brother was uncommonly handsome, with finely etched eyebrows and a strong jaw. Both parents were good-looking, though the father was fleshy with a soft chin. The article went on to enumerate the contributions that each had made to their community. I had never met any of these people, and yet I sensed a general diminishment, as if the quality of my own life was sure to suffer as a consequence of these four deaths. I felt silly as tears came into my eyes and overflowed on to my cheeks, and I quickly wiped them away. I had come to the cafeteria for coffee, which I had finished a while ago, but I remained seated, staring at the same page, the four photos. Then, before I could lower the paper and fold it up, a colleague from my department, Paula, with whom I had not spoken since the accident, joined me.

'I can barely stand to think about it,' she said as she took a seat across from me. 'It's so terrible.'

I laid the paper flat on the table, still open to the page I had been reading. 'So did you know her? Was she in any of your classes?'

Paula nodded and sipped her coffee. 'I had her in all three of my classes. So you can imagine what it's been like. It's impossible to look around the room and not think about her. And this picture,' she tapped the newspaper, 'doesn't do her justice. She was beautiful. Radiant. You couldn't help noticing her. But … You know how some women carry their beauty differently than others? Well, Anitra was beautiful in a way that was sophisticated without being flashy. Or maybe what I mean is that she was casual about it, like it wasn't important to her. She didn't build a persona around the way she looked. She let her actions do that for her.'

'Are you going to the memorial service?'

'I think we're all supposed to go. Isn't that how you read the announcement?'

I shrugged. 'I'm not sure. I didn't think it was mandatory. And since I didn't know her …'

'I think you should come. You're new and it would be a good idea for you to be seen there with the rest of us.'

I nodded and looked at the newspaper again. The moment I saw Anitra's picture my throat tightened and tears surged back into my eyes. I felt ridiculous, but Paula didn't say anything as I wiped them away. She reached across the table and turned the paper so the photograph was facing her. I watched as she regarded the dead girl's image. A faint smile appeared on her lips.

'The worst part of it for me,' she said, 'is that just before Anitra left she handed in the next assignment, a week early. Now that they're all in I'm going to have to mark them. It seems pointless, but I suppose I should give her a grade.'

'After you finish the marking what are you going to do with it?'

She looked at me. 'I don't know.'

'There must be somebody around here,' I suggested. 'A relative who's taking care of their things.'

Paula shrugged. 'I spoke to the dean. He doesn't know of anyone. She didn't live on campus, but she had a locker. He suggested putting everything in a box and taking it to their house.'

'Where did they live?'

'I'm not sure. Somewhere in the city.'

I nodded.

'So,' she said, standing up. 'Will we be seeing you at the memorial service?'

'I guess so.'

'It's a gesture, not a commitment.' She smiled. 'So, I'll see you later then.'

After she left I chanced another look at the photograph. I sensed Anitra's eyes on me. People die all the time, unexpectedly, unjustly. There's no point trying to find a reason. It just happens by chance: like dropping a pencil on the floor or catching a stranger's eye in a crowd. If Anitra Siddiqui and her family had not been on that plane, it still would have crashed. There was no pattern, no plan. Enter one door and you end up in a new country with an education and a good job. Enter another and you spend your whole life hungry, cold, and ignorant.

The service was held in the campus chapel. I arrived just as it was getting underway, and I was glad I'd followed Paula's advice, for if I had not come I would have been the only one who failed to attend. Classes had been cancelled and every office on campus was shut for the occasion. All the seats were occupied, and the rest of the space was filled with people standing. I was at the very back, against the wall. I could see little of the proceedings from this distance. A priest spoke briefly about God's plan, but since it was a nondenominational service other people were invited to speak as well. The college president said a few words, and he was followed by Anitra's friends, at least a dozen of them. After about twenty minutes it became very warm, and I had to take off my jacket. At the end someone strummed a guitar and sang, but I couldn't make out the words. I looked for Paula as we began filing out, but I didn't see her.

In the following days life on the campus resumed its scheduled routine. But there were differences. My students all seemed nervous and depressed, and it was difficult to get discussions going in class. An article on Anitra appeared in the college's weekly publication, and someone took the photo that had appeared in the newspaper, enlarged it to poster size, wrote her birth and death dates at the bottom, and taped it to the wall in the lobby of the main administration building.

Something Paula said had stayed with me as well, about the school removing Anitra's belongings from her locker and sending them to her house. The same day as our conversation I had looked up Dr Siddiqui's name in the telephone directory and found the address. But I was not familiar with the neighbourhood and the name of the street meant nothing to me. I bought a street map and put it in the glove box of my car. Then, one evening after my last class was finished, I drove to the suburb where the Siddiquis had lived.

I parked down the street and approached the house on foot. The evening had turned cool and there were not many people about. Across the street a group of boys was tossing a football. A dog was with them. Their shouts echoed sharply and the dog ran after the airborne football, barking as if at an intruder, but none of them took notice of me.

The Siddiqui house was not special at all and was rather typical of the neighbourhood. The façade was mostly clapboard painted white with brick facing along the bottom. A few flowering shrubs had been planted beneath the living-room window. The house was perched at the top of a slight incline and the lawn rolled gently down to street level. A blue Hyundai was parked in the driveway. The house was dark. The walkway and front steps were littered with carnations and roses and a large wreath – about five feet across – had been laid in the middle of the grass. After more than a week these memorial tokens were beginning to show their age, and the air smelled of decay.

I approached the front door, stepping among the rotting flowers, to read the notes that people had left. A few of these had been rendered illegible by recent rainfall, but others were preserved in plastic. 'To my best friend killed tragically, rest in peace,' I read, with no clue to which of the Siddiquis it referred. Other notes conveyed similar sentiments, some addressed to the whole family, some to individual members.

After reading the notes, I remained on the front steps. The quiet of the neighbourhood was soothing, and I felt no hurry to go anywhere. I expected that soon someone would come along and ask what I was doing here. But the fact was I didn't know what I was doing. There was no reason for me to stay. Several times I started to leave, but then changed my mind. As the minutes went by I felt a sense of liberation, as if I had established a right to be on the property. To kill time I gathered some of the fresher flowers into a small bouquet and propped it against the railing. I peered through the window of the front door, but in the gathering dark could not make out any detail. Across the street the boys were still tossing the football back and forth, but their numbers had dwindled and the dog was gone. Otherwise the street and sidewalks were empty.

I crossed the lawn to the side of the house and followed a concrete path around to the back. There was a fence, but the gate opened when I tried it, revealing an intricately landscaped and spacious back yard filled with bushes, beds of plants, and varieties of dwarf evergreens. A portion of the yard had been levelled and laid with brick to make a patio, where they kept the outdoor furniture and a portable barbecue. The fence was about seven feet high and closed in the yard on all sides. All was quiet except for the distant drone of a television and the occasional sound of a car passing in the street. I sat in one of the plastic lawn chairs. The sky dimmed and grew dark as I watched, and everywhere shadows deepened and objects lost their definition. In a short time stars became visible overhead. I heard voices from somewhere beyond the fence, a man and a woman talking. The conversation was desultory, filled with pauses. I could not make out any of the words, and yet from the tone I could tell it was not an argument or even a discussion of any topic in particular. It was as if each spoke simply to hear the voice of the other and be comforted by it. One let drop a comment, and after a moment the other picked it up. I imagined a married couple seated beneath the light of a lamp, the wife knitting, the husband reading a book, beside them an open window. Perhaps the television was on with the sound turned down.

After a while the voices of the man and woman faded into silence. Somewhere close by a dog barked. This suburban back yard was such a great distance from northern India, I wondered how often Dr Siddiqui had come outside and, looking up at the stars as I was doing now, wondered about the path that had brought him here and all the other paths he could have followed. It seemed inconceivable that I could inhabit this space at this moment. The Siddiquis had died and I was sitting in a lawn chair in their back yard. It could not possibly mean anything. And yet there seemed to be meaning, just beyond my reach.

I was annoyed when I heard that she'd found another lover, so soon after our affair ended. I thought she should have told me herself. She had lots of opportunities. We still ran into each other, because we worked and lived in the same part of the city. I would be having lunch at a restaurant and see her across the room eating with some people from her office. I noticed her in the grocery store, picking oranges from a bin and putting them into a plastic bag. I was leaving a movie once and saw her with a girlfriend in the line-up outside waiting to go in. We had talked once or twice since our breakup, but I knew she was still angry with me. It didn't seem to matter as long as she was alone. But now she had found someone else and it didn't seem fair of her to have kept this secret from me.

The day after I found out about her lover I was invited to a party, and she was there. It was crowded and I didn't see her until she was so close I could have reached out and touched her. Our eyes met, and she looked away. As the evening progressed I went around the room, studying the faces of the men, searching for one I didn't know. But they were all familiar, and after a while I realized that she had come by herself. She avoided looking at me, but I wanted to talk to her. When I said hello she only glanced at me in that cutting way she had and turned her back. I didn't recognize myself in that brief glimpse of her eyes. It seemed impossible that we had lived together for six months.

Finally, a week or so later, after seeing her on the street outside the library and again at an art exhibit, I telephoned and asked her to meet me for lunch. At first she said she was too busy, but I argued that there was no sense pretending that our time together had never happened, and, speaking for myself, I wanted us to be friends. It was obvious we were going to continue running into each other, so why not make it pleasant?

That day, as I watched her approach the table, smiling in a way that said I was the only person in the world, I was carried back to a time not long ago when to be away from her was to feel close to death, when the living warmth of her skin meant everything. I could still remember how easily she had seen through the self I presented to the world and into my heart. Somehow she had made me open up to her, and before I knew what I was doing I had told her stories about my childhood that I had never shared with anyone. The memory of her body moving beneath mine as we made love returned to me vividly, and I remembered the cry that escaped her throat at the moment of climax. I could still hear her voice as it came to me over the telephone when we were separated, and feel the craving for sexual abandon that was always just below the surface of her and which I learned how to unleash at a touch. I relived of all of this as she approached the table and took her seat. But as she said hello and looked into my eyes, and as I heard her innocent, flute-like voice speak my name, I felt nothing.

I asked all the right questions, and soon she was telling me about her new lover. I feigned interest and pretended to share her happiness. She spoke with curious animation, her hands in constant motion, her voice rising and falling. The smile never left her lips. I sat back and watched her, blocking out the words. I knew she had never spoken this way about me. Ours had not been a carefree love. At its root had been the unhealthy obsession each of us had harboured for the other.

We had first met two years before, and had taken only passing notice of each other. Our circle of friends was small, and over several months we ran into each other a dozen times under all kinds of circumstances. We were always in the company of other people and on our way somewhere. We had been introduced once, maybe twice, but her face remained hazy in my memory, and she never entered my thoughts outside of these encounters. Then, late one afternoon, I met her on the street. It was a cold day and I had just lost my job, and because I was lonely and a bit depressed I asked her to come and have a cup of coffee with me. I told her it would be my treat. She smiled and took my arm and we set off together. Suddenly nothing seemed more natural than for her to be holding my arm on a winter day with flakes of snow settling on the collar of her coat. We found a café and I ordered lattes for us both. I was afraid that once we installed ourselves across the table from one another – virtual strangers – we would have nothing to say. But my customary reserve vanished and I began telling her everything, confessing to longings I had never known I had until that moment. I spoke for an hour without pausing. In that time the afternoon light faded and dusk settled in, but she gave no sign that she wanted to leave.

Then it was her turn. She spoke intimately, about herself and her family. She described some of the things that previous lovers had done to her. I found myself attracted by her vulnerability and by the pale translucence of her skin, which hardly seemed sufficient protection in the world of shifting allegiances that we both inhabited. As we left the café I knew that I would make love to her that night. We went for something to eat, holding hands as we walked, in silence now that everything had been said. In the restaurant we both ate slowly, speaking only a word here and there. Something was emerging between us and neither of us knew what it was. Beneath the table she stroked my leg with her foot, and the wave of physical urgency that came over me was so dizzying was afraid I'd lose consciousness.

As we ate we didn't take our eyes off each other. I suppose we were watching for signs that the moment was real. Then, later, we were in her apartment, in her bed. She held nothing back. It was as if she were being touched for the first time in her life, as if I were exposing surfaces that had never before seen the light of day. She said my foreignness excited her and begged me to say filthy things to her in my native language. I felt the suppressed violence in her and with my caresses tried to bring it to the surface. She scratched and bit me, pushed me away and held me close. It was as if she didn't know what she wanted, or as if she wanted everything at once. Afterward she struggled to avoid sleep, but her eyes closed and her breathing quieted and fell into a rhythm. I lay watching her, marvelling at the gift she had given me, until I, too, fell asleep.

After that night, every parting was an agony. The hours we spent out of each other's company were endless, tedious, unendurable. When we were together, each moment sparkled, gemlike, and the only nights we didn't make love were when I was out of town or when we were too exhausted to make our bodies do the things we wanted.

It was inevitable, I suppose, that a love that blazed with this kind of intensity would soon burn itself out.

Not long after our first night together I gave up my apartment and moved in with her.

A month or so later she confronted me and said I was suffocating her. She claimed my emotional demands were unreasonable and that she would never be able to satisfy me. She accused me of trying to monopolize her affections and keep her apart from her other friends. She said I was greedy and possessive. When we fought, our disgust for each other was proportional to our love. At first, our disagreements concluded with anger, tears, then passionate reconciliations, and for a while our love would shine all the brighter. But as time went on there were more slammed doors, more embarrassing scenes in restaurants. The animal physicality of our lovemaking spilled over into our arguments, and in time we both bore scars, which we concealed beneath long-sleeved sweaters and high collars. At a party given by a colleague of mine she accused me of flirting with the wife of our host, and when I denied it and told her she was crazy she slapped my face in front of everyone. What came next was a long silence while we looked into each other's eyes. We went home without speaking a word. We both understood that we were finished. I moved out the next morning while it was still dark, before she woke up, before we could make our apologies. A few days later I sent a friend over to collect my things. I couldn't face her. I was afraid that the love we had cherished would be the end of us both if we went on reviving and nourishing it.

For several weeks nothing passed between us. I did not see her and did not try to contact her. I found another place to live and it wasn't long before I let my friends convince me that it was time to start going out to bars and restaurants again.

The first time I saw her I felt like the floor was falling away underneath me and I was being sucked into a vortex. I couldn't even tell if what I felt was love or hate. At that moment I realized that we had allowed our identity as a couple to obliterate us as individuals, so that

I felt lost and naked on my own. The sight of her in the company of other people humiliated me. However, over time, after encountering her on a regular basis and even speaking to her briefly on a couple of occasions, repetition dulled my response so that when I saw her out with her friends, it seemed to me that I felt nothing.

After lunch we had coffee. She was still talking about her lover. I let her go on. When it was time to leave I smiled and told her it was wonderful to see her. On the sidewalk in front of the restaurant we embraced. I watched her walk away and turn the corner. Then I used a public telephone to call the school where I was teaching. I told the secretary I'd been taken ill and would not be back that afternoon. After that I went to the bank where her lover worked.

He was a clerk. From her description I knew immediately which one he was.

I joined the queue. At one point I stepped out of the line when it became clear that he was being delayed by a lengthy transaction. But I worked out the timing, and when I reached the front of the queue, his wicket was the next one to come free.

He greeted me cordially, with a smile and a brief comment on the weather. Otherwise his manner was impersonal – businesslike and professional. I kept him occupied for about fifteen minutes with the complexities of opening an account and transferring funds from one of my other accounts into the new one. It took him a while to complete the paperwork and to obtain verification that the transfer had cleared, and during this time I was able to observe him. He was fleshy, with soft porous skin and an unnatural sheen to his black hair that made it look as if he had just stepped out of the shower. He had a goatee and a neatly cropped moustache. His plum-coloured tie, flecked with gold, was a perfect match for his burgundy shirt. On the middle finger of his right hand was a large signet ring, possibly a family heirloom. His hands were large and soft and the skin at the knuckles was dimpled like a child's. When he left his station to get a signature or to carry out some other piece of business, he stood straight as he walked. His belt cut tautly into the flesh at his waist. My knowledge of him was making me light-headed. Every time I imagined him in bed with her my chest muscles hardened and my neck grew warm.

When we were done he smiled and handed me my new bank-book, holding it open at the front page where the balance was clearly displayed. I thanked him and took a seat in the waiting area.

I was leafing through a magazine a short while later when another young man arrived and relieved him at his station. I watched as her lover removed his jacket from the back of the chair and said a few words to a female colleague. Then he disappeared into a back room.

I stood in line once again. At the wicket I handed the clerk – this time a young woman – my new bankbook and told her that I wanted to close the account. She seemed perplexed when she glanced through it and found only a single entry, dated that day, but to keep her from asking questions I told her that when she had finished closing the account I wanted to see the manager. She lowered her gaze and did not look me in the eye again as she silently carried out her duties. After presenting me with a bank draft for the account balance she hurried off and returned with another woman, who smiled as she asked me to accompany her.

I was shown into a small office. In a few moments a stocky man with sweat on his upper lip and wearing a grey suit bustled in and asked how he could help me.

He sat down and stared at me but was unable to maintain eye contact for more than a few seconds at a stretch. He seemed preoccupied and kept checking his watch.

I explained that I had opened a personal account and that I had intended to bring my business accounts here as well. But the young man who had handled the transaction had been surly and abrupt, and so I had decided not to carry through with my original plan and had, in fact, closed out the personal account immediately. I wanted nothing further to do with this bank, but I was taking time out of my day to let him know what had happened and to tell him that I didn't think it was wise to place people like that in positions where a bad first impression could mean the difference between keeping business and losing it.

His apology was effusive. When he asked which of the clerks had offended me I gave him a detailed description.

He thanked me and I left.

Outside, the air had turned chilly and seemed to suggest that snow might fall, though the sky was clear. I crossed the street and went into a fast-food restaurant. I ordered a coffee, which I took to a table by the window where I could enjoy a clear view of the street. Perhaps twenty minutes later, her lover emerged from the bank. He descended the steps and, apparently undecided about what his next move should be, looked around with a puzzled air. He held his gloves together in one hand and stood idly slapping them against his other hand. I thought he might turn and go back in, but after a thoughtful moment he began walking rapidly. He appeared to be talking to himself and his face was flushed. In his hurry he dropped one of his gloves, but a man in a trench coat called his attention to this, and he reversed his steps to retrieve it. He and the man exchanged a few words and both were smiling when they parted.

It was a meaningless act of courtesy, the kind that strangers often perform for one another, and yet I felt warmed and elated at having brought this connection about.

The gallery was on Nikos Street, across from the English bookstore and just down from a busy travel agent's office. The invitation was for seven in the evening. I didn't want to be the first to arrive, so I went into the bookstore and spent a few moments browsing the shelves. Among the patrons were some American tourists. A woman in blue shorts, with thick legs and wearing running shoes, held a plastic basket filled with paperbound romance novels. In the fiction section a little girl was reading the titles on the spines of the books. She wore a white cotton dress and her straw-blond hair had been braided into pigtails.

I selected a book from the shelf and opened the cover.

'A. Sport. Of. Nature,' the girl read. 'The. Con. Conser. Conservat.'

'Conservationist,' said the woman.

The girl glanced up at the woman, whom I took to be her mother. She didn't seem to mind the interruption. Without speaking she turned back to the books.

'Burger's. Daughter. A. World. Of. Strangers.'

'That's very good,' I said.

'Andrea, please be quiet. You're bothering the other people.' The woman spoke sharply.

'No, she's not,' I said.

Looking up at me, Andrea seemed to realize suddenly that she was in a public place. She retreated to her mother's side, and, taking the woman by the hand, looked at me solemnly.

I smiled and waved to her as I left the fiction section and went up the stairs to the travel books. I found one on China and was looking at some photographs of the Yangtze River when I noticed Andrea at the top of the stairs, watching me. Her expression didn't change when I smiled at her, so I turned back to the book. A minute later I could still feel her staring at me. I smiled again, but I didn't know what she wanted and couldn't think of anything to say. I returned the book to its place on the shelf and moved away from her down the aisle.

I spent another ten minutes leafing through the pages of books. Andrea was nowhere in sight when I left to go across the street.

I showed my invitation to the girl at the door and stepped inside. I had been to the Gallery Atticus on three other occasions, and as I made my way through the noisy crowd to the hors d'oeuvres table a couple of people nodded to me. Many of those present looked familiar, in that shadowy manner of people you do not see often. One whom I'd never seen before was a man wearing a rumpled corduroy jacket. He appeared to be in his early fifties. His thinning hair was unkempt and he was paunchy, almost overweight. But he had a kind face. He was clean-shaven and wore rounded gold-rimmed spectacles. He smiled at me across the table as I loaded a plate with boiled shrimp, assorted canapés, and vegetables with dip, and accepted a glass of white wine from the bartender. I returned his smile but did not let my gaze linger.

I turned my back to the crowd of art lovers and pushed the food into my mouth. I chewed as quickly as I could and chased it with half the glass of wine. I took another mouthful. Once the gnawing in my stomach had eased and I'd filled my plate a second time, I turned to look at the paintings.

I had not bothered to read the invitation in detail and had only taken note of the fact that the exhibit was showcasing the work of a group, not a single artist. The first painting that drew my attention was at least eight feet wide and dominated the entire end of the room. It was a reproduction of Da Vinci's *Last Supper*, rendered realistically and in detail. Like most people, I knew the original only from books, and so the work before me seemed an accurate representation of Da Vinci's masterpiece, except that all the figures were naked. The effect was startling and suggested that the apostles' horror did not result from the fact that Jesus had just declared one of them a traitor, but from their lack of clothes, as if they'd just removed blinders from their eyes and were shocked to find themselves at a table of naked men. The calm face of Jesus, who sat with his slender white arms spread before him, seemed not godly but wanton, and the others, with their muscles bulging and their chest hairs bristling, seemed hardly able to contain their anger.

I was unable to conceal my surprise. I stood gawking, my mouth open and full of half-chewed food. Other people stood about as well, but they seemed to regard the painting with bland amusement. Quite close to me two young women in long dresses exchanged confidential whispers that left them smiling and giggling. Further along some young men gestured toward the painting as they appeared to discuss the skill of the artist.

I had finished my second plate of food and returned to the table for a third helping. By this time the room was getting crowded. There were no shrimp left. I had to be satisfied with triangles of pita bread with hummus and a few pieces of green and red pepper and broccoli with dip, and another glass of wine. The last time I had come to this gallery they had served sweets and coffee after the public ceremony was finished.

I wanted to stay away from the other end of the room, where a microphone had been fitted into a stand. This is where everyone's attention would be focused once the time came for speeches and introductions. My status as an interloper was plain enough, but there was no need to place myself within the line of sight of all the assembled guests. I wove my way through the throng of bodies until I reached the rear of the gallery space, near an emergency exit. Here was another painting, no less startling than the Da Vinci copy. It was a madonna with child, again painted in an antiquated style such as an Italian or Dutch Renaissance master would have used. Mary cradled the baby in her arms partially wrapped in a cloth. However, her expression was not of blissful adoration, as we expect in such works, but one of stunned amazement. Her mouth was open and her eyes were trained on the child's penis, which stood erect, surrounded by a bristly thicket of pubic hair.

I grew warm and looked away. For a minute or two I kept my head down and studied the floor. I was not religious, I had no politics, no aesthetic tastes to speak of. But these works struck me not only as offensive, but deliberately so. Finally I raised my eyes. The gallery was filled. People were busy viewing the paintings and making conversation and laughing. Nobody seemed in the least troubled. I moved down the line to another painting. It depicted a family seated at a dinner table. Something about the hairstyles and furnishings suggested America in the 1950s. Everyone was smiling, and in this regard it was like an advertisement in a magazine from that era depicting a perfect moment of domestic harmony. But again, the artist had introduced an element of perversity. The table divided the view into halves. Above the table we had a normal family enjoying a meal and conversing about the day's events. Below the table everyone was naked. The husband and son were masturbating and the mother and daughter had their hands between their legs, which were spread wide apart.

'It makes you think, doesn't it?'

'I'm sorry?'

The man in the rumpled jacket stood behind me. He gestured toward the painting with the hand that held his wineglass.

'I'm sorry. I didn't mean to startle you. But it makes you think. About what's really going on in people's minds. He's not afraid to bring it to our attention.'

'I'm not sure I care to be reminded of such things,' I said.

'Well, yes. There are people who feel that way. Life is troubling enough. Why expose our basest instincts to public scrutiny?'

I didn't answer. I would have left him to contemplate the painting on his own, but the crowd was so thick that pushing past all these people would have drawn a great deal of attention.

'I've been watching you, you know.'

I looked at him, more closely this time.

'Are you an artist?' he asked.

'Are you?'

'I asked you first.'

He smiled. Or, I should say, he had not stopped smiling. He had large teeth, stained yellow by coffee or tobacco. His nose was prominent and hooked slightly to the left. I did not like his curiosity, but his interest in me seemed casual rather than official. I did not feel threatened. As I studied his face he swayed slightly on his feet, and I thought maybe he was drunk, though probably he had been jostled by the crowd milling about behind him. Whatever the case, he seemed to regard me kindly. I felt it was unlikely that he would cause me trouble.

'I'm a student,' I said. 'I'm studying art history.' In these surroundings, this lie seemed an appropriate one.

'Well, if you don't mind my saying, you're going to have to adjust your attitude if you intend to become a scholar of art history. There's worse than this out there.'

'I know what I like,' I said. 'And this isn't it.'

'You should know by now that liking and disliking are not in themselves valid responses. We have to be able to say why. If we can't say why, then we have no right to hold an opinion.'

His statement left little room for argument. I turned back to the painting of the family.

'Why have you been watching me?'

He laughed, but quickly caught himself and became serious. 'Please, don't get the wrong impression. I'm too impulsive sometimes.' He shook his head. 'It gets the better of me and I just make a fool of myself. But, you know, I see something, and it grabs me.' Out of the corner of my eye I saw him emphatically grasp the empty air and make his hand into a fist. 'When I saw you it was like we had already met. Something in your eyes. Your posture. I saw myself at twenty, alone in a big city, waiting for things to happen. I know it sounds strange, but I had a story about you in my mind from that first moment.'

I turned to him again. 'You know nothing about me.'

'I know, I know,' he said, gesturing again with the wineglass. 'It sounds odd, doesn't it? I'm casting you in a role. That's what I'm doing. I don't even know your name and here I am declaring that I can tell you things about yourself that even you don't know. It's preposterous. Forgive me.'

He kept his eyes on me and smiled in a fashion that seemed apologetic, even humble. Whatever was going on here, I seemed to have gained the upper hand. There was something of desperation in his manner. He did not want to offend me.

'Such as?'

'For that, my young friend, you will have to wait. Duty calls. You will stay, I hope. Won't you? For the rest of the evening?'

I had planned to leave the moment my stomach was filled. However, I had lately been spending almost all of my time alone, and his offer of companionship was attractive. The conversation, if steered away from the personal and toward the abstract, promised to become interesting. I bowed my head slightly.

'Bravo, then! I will see you later.'

I had to step forward to keep him in view as he squeezed his way through the crowd toward the microphone. His body was thick through the middle and one would have thought him ungainly, and yet he moved lightly on his feet. At the front of the room he spoke to a young woman who was adjusting the height of the stand. A few moments later the crowd had quieted and, as she started to speak, turned to listen. I left my empty plate on a table and accepted another glass of wine from a passing waiter.

She introduced him as Jonah Keller, professor of art history from the Rilke Institute in Berlin. He looked at the floor and fidgeted like a bored child as she enumerated his credentials, mentioned titles of books he had written, and listed the shows he had organized and the universities where he had taught. But when she had finished and people were clapping politely, he moved forward with a confident step.

With one hand on the microphone he spoke about contemporary art and the importance of images in our daily lives. We live in a society of images, he said. Everyone is trying to get our attention and they use images to do it. Memorable images – memorable because they are pleasing or memorable because they are disturbing – lodge themselves in our memory, impossible to forget. This has been empirically verified, in tests in which receptors attached to the skull measure the degree and type of stimulation certain images create in different parts of the brain. The more familiar the image, the more meaning we attach to it, and the more activity is triggered in the brain's cognitive centres. It is interesting to note, he said, that aversion and disgust, and delight and joy, trigger exactly the same kinds of brain activity. Which raises the issue of whether these reactions are caused by the image itself, or by conditioning we have received throughout our lives, or by some sort of instinctual reflex of which we are unaware. In other words, our response to beauty and ugliness remains a mystery. Who, he asked, can say with certainty what is truly beautiful and what is truly ugly? We can analyze the image and determine to our satisfaction if it is good art. But we cannot break down its beauty into component parts, for beauty resides in qualities that are impossible to define. Undoubtedly we derive pleasure from beauty, and in this way take an approximate measure of its worth. But once again, pleasure does not allow itself to be quantified. This is why words like 'beautiful' and 'ugly' are not helpful when it comes to discussing art. They are, believe it or not, he said, beside the point. What we are left with, once the gaze has moved on to the next picture, is the image. Always the image. No more, no less.

After a significant pause he went on in this vein for another few minutes. His voice was deeply resonant and, helped along by the sound system, projected its authoritative tones into every corner of the room. People around me were nodding. I had never thought about this sort of thing before and could only assume he was right. What he was saying seemed to make sense. More fascinating to me, however, was that there were people who could make a living thinking and talking about these issues. They inhabited a world I had never suspected was out there.

It wasn't long before he was introducing the artists. All four were young and dark-haired. They'd dressed casually in jackets and jeans, and looked so much alike they could have been brothers. They came from Prague and had names like Lazlo and Joska and Jascha. Keller said they were exponents of the new 'adaptive' style, which, as he explained, meant they took familiar images and twisted them to suit their own purposes. As he spoke, they stood behind him in a row with their hands folded in front of them. One scowled, another smiled. Their faces expressed something between pleasure and pain. By this time I was on my fifth glass of wine, and as Professor Keller finished his speech I concentrated on solving the mystery of why he had singled me out. Like the featured artists I was young. I was also unattached, and my poverty was evident in the poor cut of my clothes. Maybe he was taking pity on me. Or perhaps his attraction was sexual and he thought I would comply with his wishes if he offered enough money. Whatever his intentions, he had aroused my curiosity.

When he finished speaking and declared the exhibit open, a new round of applause rose from those assembled. I let my gaze wander around the room. A few of the young women were wearing high heels, full-length evening dresses, and diamond jewellery. Some of the men wore expensive suits. But a large number had either chosen – or, like me, been reduced to – outfits that were barely serviceable: faded jeans, mismatched socks, threadbare jackets, bare feet in sandals. I had purchased my shirt at a flea market, three for a dollar. As I watched, Jonah Keller circulated and exchanged greetings with an assortment of women both young and old, an elderly gentleman, and some young men. He was equally at ease shaking the hand of a rich benefactor, or huddled in earnest conversation with an artist apparently hungry for both nourishment and recognition.

As I roamed the gallery I took more wine whenever a waiter happened by and did my best to finish off the last scraps of food. Every painting I looked at was repellent on some level. I saw no merit in any of them, unless shock value was a quality that deserved praise. After an hour or so I felt a hand on my elbow as I contemplated a painting of a horse with grotesquely swollen, and conspicuously human, genitalia. Keller was at my side. He drew me away from the painting and whispered, 'I'm ready to leave if you are. We can continue our conversation over coffee if you like. The paintings will be here for a few weeks if you want to come back and see them when the gallery's less crowded.'

I drained my glass and left it on a table. The coffee and sweets were just being brought out, but I was happy to miss them this time. In all, I had drunk seven or eight glasses of wine, and was conscious of a tingling sensation in my extremities and a bit of light-headedness.

But I still felt steady on my feet.

As we approached the exit Keller made his apologies for leaving early to several of the young women who had been circulating about the room all evening, one of them the woman who had introduced him. Each gave me a curious glance, as it was obvious we were leaving together. But he didn't seem bothered by this and didn't offer to introduce me.

The sky was dotted with stars and the night air balmy. Keller set off in the direction of the Acropolis, which was lit up like a sculpture on a pedestal. I fell into step beside him as if nothing could be more natural.

'The most that can be said for these events is that they expose you to new trends. But one grows weary of all this striving to be provocative, all these attempts to stir up controversy. After a while it becomes unseemly.'

'So you weren't impressed?'

He reached into an inner pocket of his jacket and drew out a package of cigarettes. They were Greek, unfiltered. He flipped it open and offered it to me. I took one.

'It's not a matter of being impressed. Technically, they're masters at what they do. It's beyond dispute. You have to look very closely to find any sort of flaw. It's just that after all the fuss, one wonders if what they do is worth doing.'

'Are you saying you didn't like those paintings?'

We paused as he lit his own cigarette and then mine. To cut down on expenses I had stopped buying cigarettes. I had not smoked in months, and the coarse aromatic smoke flooded my lungs and made my eyes water. It was all I could do to keep from coughing.

'I told you, it's not my job to like or dislike anything. These people have talent and should be encouraged. Maybe today they're producing trash, but who knows what they'll be doing ten, twenty, thirty years from now?'

'I thought your job was to judge the value of the work. To pronounce it worthy if that's what you felt.'

He waved his hand dismissively. 'If I've disappointed you I'm sorry, but I leave such pronouncements to the press. Let them go out on a limb. I've been criticized too often for bestowing praise indiscriminately. One of the women who own that gallery is a former student, so when she invited me, I came. I did my duty. No one can fault me for that.'

Keller turned a corner and I followed, more or less blindly. I had assumed we would go to a café and continue our chat over an aperitif, but he was leading me away from the restaurant district. Instinct told me he was harmless, but the wine had muddied my thinking a bit. I really had no idea what he thought about anything, including me. He was a snob. That much was clear. But was he also a hypocrite, foisting art that he thought was garbage on an unsuspecting public? Did he regard the whole business as nothing more than a huge joke?

Ahead of us I saw some people walking and when I recognized the woman's blue shorts and stocky legs, and the girl's white dress and blond pigtails, I realized they were the American family from the bookstore, Andrea and her mother. They both carried full shopping bags. It was after ten o'clock, late for a child to be walking the streets of a big city. We were almost past them when I heard the mother's voice.

'Excuse me.' Keller turned.

'Yes?'

'Oh, you speak English! Thank God!' As she rested her bags on the ground and unfolded a map of the city, Andrea turned and looked at me. There was no surprise in her expression, nothing to indicate she thought it odd that we would encounter one another again so soon. She regarded me with the same stony, unflinching gaze as before.

'This city,' the mother said. 'It makes no sense at all. I don't know why we came.'

'Is there some way I can be of assistance?' Keller asked.

'I'm trying to find our hotel. The Attallos. It's on Athinas Street.' She poked her finger at the map. 'Here. But I don't know where we are. The streets go every which way.'

Smiling, Keller lifted the map out of her hands. His placid manner had a calming effect on her. She drew in a deep breath and placed one hand over her heart.

'This street,' he said, indicating where we stood with a sweeping gesture, 'is just here.' He held the map where she could see it and, pointing, moved his finger along its surface in a straight line. 'Athinas runs perpendicular. You are very close. You have only to continue down this way and at the corner turn to your right.'

'To the right?' she asked, looking from Keller to the map, then back to him as if unable to comprehend what he was saying.

He extended his arm to indicate the street on which we stood.

'Down here to the very end,' he said, speaking slowly. 'Turn right, and you will find the street you are looking for.'

He folded the map over and gave it back to her.

'I sure hope you're right,' she said with a sigh. 'We've been walking in circles for an hour. My feet are so sore.' She completed the job of folding the map into a small rectangle and took up her bags. 'Thank you. You're very kind. Say thank you to the man, Andrea.'

Andrea shifted her eyes away from me and smiled at Keller.

'Thank you,' she said.

When they were out of sight he took the package of cigarettes from his pocket and again offered me one before taking one for himself. As he lit them he said, 'That poor girl will be lost for the rest of her life. We're going this way.'

We entered a slightly inclined side street narrower than the one we'd left. Keller marched ahead of me and I almost tripped over my own feet trying to keep up. Because the sidewalk was crowded with parked cars, we were forced to walk in the middle of the cobbled lane. There was nobody around. The echo of our steps created a hollow clatter against the darkened façades of the squat apartment buildings lining the street.

'What is your name?' he asked after we had been silent for some minutes.

'Kostandin. Kostandin Bitri.'

'Well, Kostandin, now that we know each other better I hope you will call me Jonah.'

'Thank you,' I said.

'And, if you will bear with me, I will tell you the story that came to me when I saw you.' He stopped walking. 'I don't believe you are a student. You don't have that look about you, the look that says you're hungry for knowledge. You are intelligent, but it isn't a schooled intelligence. Also, you were alone tonight. In my experience students always travel in groups or pairs.' He waved his hand, dismissing his own words this time. 'But this doesn't mean a thing. I don't want to sound critical. You aren't a student, but you would be if you could afford it. The important thing now is that you learn. Listen and learn.'

He smiled.

'You have lost contact with your family.'

For a second or two I could not believe I had heard correctly. But his smile calmed me. I nodded.

'It's always unfortunate when that happens,' he said as he resumed walking, 'no matter what the circumstances. I won't speculate about your situation. You can tell me about it some other time. In my own case, their plans for me differed from my own. The break was inevitable, and when it came, I found myself, like you, alone in the city waiting for something to happen. Eventually it did. I take it you have not heard from any of your relatives for a long time.'

'Yes.'

'You have my condolences. This is a great loss, perhaps in your case a tragic loss. Sometimes it will seem more than you can bear. But I am living proof that it's possible to survive. You and I, Kostandin, we're very much alike. I'm not clairvoyant. Everything I'm telling you is in your eyes. I've seen that look before. It stared at me from the mirror for years. Forgive me for being blunt, but you'll never get over the loss of your family. This kind of trauma marks a person for life. But I can see you want to make something of yourself, so you must harden your heart and move on.'

I made no response. Earlier, I had assumed that everything he said was right, but now that he was talking about me and not art, I wasn't so sure. However, I couldn't say with confidence that he was wrong either. Maybe he wanted me to argue with him. But he spoke with such authority, every word that came from his mouth seemed like pure truth.

As we walked I sensed him glancing at me sidelong.

'Tonight,' he said, 'I think you were as attracted to me as I was to you. You came with me because I represent what you have lost. I give you hope.'

Again I nodded. I could not deny this either because apart from simple companionship, it had occurred to me that he might be able to help me. He didn't dress like it, but I was sure he came from money. He seemed to have international connections. Briefly, I entertained a hope that he hadn't noticed the selfishness that was at the root of my actions. But this hope faded quickly, and all I was left with was the strangeness of having the layers stripped away and my motives dissected, and with such ease by someone I'd only just met. I wanted to hate him for what he was doing. But his manner – that of someone simply reporting the facts without a trace of smugness or impertinence – made this impossible.

'You may appreciate art, but you were there tonight for the food. I could see this easily enough and I don't think I was the only one. You are uncomfortable in rooms that are full of people. I don't blame you for that. It takes a long time to stop feeling like an outsider. You believe on the one hand that people should accept you as you are, but on the other hand you suspect they're waiting for you to make a mistake so they can throw you out. The world is fickle. You're right to be suspicious. This is why you didn't talk to anyone, and you wouldn't have had I not spoken to you first. Your English is good but it could be better. If you allow me, I'll help you to improve it. Here we are.'

He produced a set of keys and unlocked the door of an apartment building with a peeling stucco façade. The door was decorated with iron grillwork and featured four panes of privacy glass arranged in a row at eye level. Inside, the floors and staircase were of polished marble. He led the way up the stairs, and on the first landing, where a vase holding an arrangement of roses, irises, and anemones stood on a small table beneath an ornate mirror, unlocked one of the three apartment doors.

'Please,' he said, standing back to allow me to enter.

I went in. Behind me, Jonah switched on the light. The apartment was not extravagantly appointed but was filled with objects, among them books that fully occupied five floor-to-ceiling bookcases. The furnishings were plain, functional. A beige sofa faced a television. A wooden dining table with six chairs sat in an alcove just off the small kitchen. The walls had been painted a peculiar hue of faded tomato red and were covered with framed photographs and rows of small paintings. Several rugs, possibly Persian or else good imitations, concealed most of the wooden floor. Shelf after shelf was laden with knick-knacks of every description. A darkened hallway led to other rooms. Occupying a stuffed chair in the corner was a large orange cat. He lifted his head briefly as we entered, but otherwise took no notice of us.

Jonah went into the kitchen.

'Please, Kostandin, have a seat. In case you're wondering, this is my sister's apartment. She teaches classical literature here at the university; hence the abundance of books. As you can see, she collects things, though I don't find her collecting has much rhyme or reason to it. If she likes something, she buys it. Much like me, I'm afraid. She's not here at the moment.'

I sat on the sofa. While we were walking I had felt fine, but now all I wanted was to lie down and go to sleep. I closed my eyes and listened to the sounds coming from the kitchen: the clink of glass, the cork pulled from a bottle, the fresh flow of liquid being poured.

'You're tired,' Jonah said. Suddenly he was standing above me holding two glasses of white wine. 'You should see a doctor. You're probably malnourished.'

He pushed a glass into my hand and sat across from me in an upholstered chair. There was a low square table between us. Soft piano music was coming from a set of speakers. I wondered how long it had been playing.

'I don't know what you think I can do for you,' I said. 'If you want me to go to bed with you, I won't do it. Not for any amount of money?'

He waved his hand.

'You're right to be suspicious. My motives are a puzzle, even to me.' He leaned forward, both hands wrapped around his glass, elbows on his knees. 'I was married once. We were both academics and we were always travelling. It seemed we were never home at the same time. It didn't work out and we divorced. I've always regretted the failure of my marriage because I believe I would make a good father. I wish I had had a son. Someone I could share my experience with, who would appreciate my advice. You know how it is. In the years I've been teaching, my protégés have been my sons. I've helped mould them and shape their intellects. But like all children they move away; they get jobs in other countries, and I never hear from them again. I suppose I'm hoping that in you I've found another opportunity to make something substantial from the raw material at hand.' He laughed silently. 'It's pure arrogance, I admit. And it's risky too. I really know nothing about you and maybe I shouldn't trust you. Or maybe I'll find you don't have what it takes to do what I ask of you. I admit I've been mistaken before. But I can't help myself. When I saw you tonight I thought, here is someone who is lost. He needs to build a new identity, but he lacks the means and perhaps even the imagination to do it. You can't go home, because home doesn't exist any more. By some fluke you find yourself in a city on the Mediterranean where opportunities are plentiful, but because you are neither the person you were nor the person you want to be, these opportunities pass you by.'

We sipped our wine in silence. Jonah settled into his chair. I waited for him to go on.

'The older I get the more I think about the work I still have to do and less about the work I've completed. It's my legacy that worries me now. By the standards of western society I'm still a young man, but my father died of a heart attack at forty-five. I'm an American, but I've spent most of my adult life in Europe. Nobody at home knows who I am. Here, I can walk into any institute for the humanities and have people salivating at the prospect of hearing me speak. Over there my name means nothing and my opinions less. It's only through people like you that I will create something lasting. If I can use my influence to open doors for you, doors you would otherwise find closed, the only reward I ask is the chance to watch you make a success of yourself and know that I helped in some small way.' He smiled. He was no longer looking at me. His gaze had turned vague and seemed to fall in the vicinity of the tabletop. I was beginning to wonder if he was mad. 'You know, I think of death a great deal. Not to be morbid, but it's all around us, as you are well aware. I sometimes think that the room we will die in has already been built and that we spend our lives searching for it. Everything we do moves us nearer to that threshold. And someday we will step over it.'

I had finished my wine. With elaborate care I placed the glass on the table. My head whirled.

'But look. I'm wearing you out with all this talk. I apologize. I tend to lecture rather than engage in conversation, one of my less admirable traits, as my former wife never tires of reminding me. Tomorrow you will tell me about your life and where you come from, and, if it's not too painful, about your family and what happened to them. I must know everything if, as the expression goes, I'm to take you under my wing.'

'I'm grateful for your interest,' I began, but the idea I had been formulating dissolved before I could turn it into words. When I tried to stand I lost my balance and fell backward into the soft welcoming upholstery of the sofa.

'Tell me,' he said, leaning forward again and staring at me intently. 'Where you are living, is there someone waiting for you to come back? A woman? A cat?' He smiled. 'A plant that will die if you don't water it tonight?'

'No,' I admitted, feeling I should be angry since he seemed to be mocking me. But the anger did not materialize. Instead, I laughed.

'Then there's no reason for you to go.' He slapped his hands against his knees as if the matter were settled. 'I'll get some sheets and a blanket and make you a bed here. I think you will sleep soundly. I always sleep better when I know there's someone else close by. The bathroom is just down the hall.'

He turned on a light and bustled around for a moment, straightening things. I got to my feet and staggered in the direction of the bathroom, shedding my jacket as I went and letting it fall to the floor. As I rounded the corner my foot bumped the leg of a chair, and I saw him glance at me, afraid perhaps that I might bang into a shelf or a table and damage some of his sister's precious trinkets. I steadied myself and continued on.

In the bathroom I turned on a light and avoided looking at myself in the mirror. Almost unconsciously I unzipped my pants and emptied my bladder. I was sweating and suddenly aware that the apartment was very warm. And this in turn led me to consider these new surroundings and the fact that I did not belong here. It was a woman's bathroom, scented with powders and adorned with wallpaper featuring a delicate floral motif. On the counter by the sink was a little basket that held miniature soaps, each in its own frilly package. I turned my thoughts back to a few hours ago and tried to recount the stages in the journey that had brought me here, but my attempt to retrace my steps failed. I could see the bookstore and the American mother and daughter, and the gallery, and my encounter with Jonah, but the link with the present moment was tenuous. At some point tonight I had placed my unconditional trust in someone I knew nothing about. But I could not remember making the decision to do this, or to follow him here. My progress from my boardinghouse sitting room to this apartment seemed nothing more than a dream, as impossible as it was inevitable. I was inclined to believe what he told me, but on another level I knew that anything could happen. I was not afraid but also not tempted by Jonah's offer to tutor me and make me into something he could show off to his friends. It seemed if there were benefits to be had from this arrangement, they would be mine and nobody else's, but I was also certain I would be asked to give something up, if not tonight, then tomorrow, or the day after that. Where I come from, you don't get something for nothing.

I met my eyes in the mirror and turned away. Jonah was at the door, which I'd just noticed was ajar.

'Is everything all right in there?'

'Yes, I'm fine.' I flushed the toilet.

'You were being so quiet,' he said, retreating, 'I was afraid you had slipped away.'

I washed my hands and slapped some water on my face, but when I stepped into the hallway everything began to spin.

My jacket was hanging on the coat rack. Jonah had placed a pillow at one end of the sofa and laid out a blanket. I heard street noises and saw that a window was open. Without warning Jonah's hand was gripping my elbow. I was overcome with weariness and wanted nothing more than to slip down that sweet slope into unconsciousness.

'I understand your predicament,' he said, leading me to the sofa. 'You're having second thoughts about my offer. You don't know what I really want from you. I'll tell you the truth. I don't know what I want. I don't know why I'm doing this. You appeal to me. That's all I can say.'

Like a sick child I let him remove my shoes, settle me into a reclining position on the sofa, and pull the blanket over me. I looked into his face, which hovered above me for a second before withdrawing into the shadows.

'We will talk about it tomorrow,' he said. 'Perhaps by then we'll both be thinking more clearly.'

Suddenly it was dark. My eyes were open. For a moment I didn't know where I was, but then I remembered. I must have slept for several hours. It was the middle of the night. But this city never rests, and the clamorous echo of traffic and voices wafted in through the window. My head throbbed. In my mind the apartment as it would look in daylight appeared before me, and I wondered how many of those trinkets I could fit into my pockets and how much they would bring at a pawnshop. There was also Jonah's wallet. He would have money, credit cards. I saw myself cashing it all in at the bank, making enormous withdrawals from the automatic teller.

Then a sound distracted me, brought me back to where I was. I recalled the cat on the chair and at the same instant flinched at the impact of four feet on my chest. Purring, he turned and lay down, pinning me to the spot. A tentative paw touched my nose, then my chin. I lifted my hand and drew it down the length of the cat's bony spine. I scratched behind his ears. He nudged his muzzle against my fingers, asking for more. But I could feel my grasp on consciousness loosening. A minute later I slept.

I was working with Professor Irving Spelmann at the City University. He was an emeritus professor in the sociology department, famous for his work on symbiotic communal relationships.

When Darlene, the department chair's administrative secretary, showed me into his office, Spelmann glanced up, levelled a scowl, and grunted. 'They told me I didn't have to deal with students,' he said and turned back to the papers on his desk.

Darlene explained, 'Mr Bitri is your new research assistant.'

'How do you do, sir?' I said. I held out my hand.

He ignored me. Addressing Darlene, he asked, 'What do I want with a research assistant?'

She smiled as if half embarrassed and half amused. Her glance flickered briefly in my direction. 'We go through this every year,' she said. 'He's not as fierce as he seems. And don't worry. He works his research assistants to death.' She had Mediterranean blood: olive skin and dark hair and eyes.

Spelmann grunted again. Without looking up he commented, 'I'd appreciate it if you didn't talk about me as if I wasn't in the room.'

'I'll leave you two to get to know each other,' she said, swivelling nimbly on her heel and leaving the office. I listened as her steps receded down the length of the hallway.

Spelmann grunted occasionally but said nothing as he continued to peruse the densely typeset page, which he now held in his hand. His hair and eyebrows were unruly and snow white. He was clean-shaven and was not wearing glasses.

During this moment of reprieve, I had a chance to examine the small cluttered office: boxes on the floor with papers spilling out of them, crammed bookshelves, cobwebs. Above me a rusty water pipe emerged from a hole in the wall, turned ninety degrees at an elbow joint, and entered the ceiling. A computer, sitting on a wheeled trolley, had been pushed into a corner, its screen to the wall. There was an odour that I associated with cellar rot and old socks. Behind vertical blinds, floor-to-ceiling windows afforded a view of the main quad, which on this autumn day was dreary and wet and covered with fallen leaves. My eye was drawn to a pair of metal crutches with elbow braces leaning against a filing cabinet.

'Is there anything I can do for you, sir?' I asked. I had met his type before and was not intimidated – old men getting by on bluster and bad manners who seem to think that if they accept help without appearing to resist they are admitting a weakness.

'Sit down,' he said. 'You're making me nervous, standing there like a butler.'

I sat and waited as he continued to read.

'What do you know about my theories?' He shot the question at me like a missile.

'Nothing, sir,' I said.

Now he raised his eyes, which were a vivid green. 'And why do you think you were assigned to me?'

'I can't say, sir. I never have any luck with these things.'

The corner of his mouth twitched.

'Another one of their jokes, eh? You're not from around here.'

'That's right, sir.'

He tilted his head.

'You're from one of those countries over there that used to be part of Yugoslavia. I'm right, aren't I? How many languages do you speak?'

'Seven fluently, sir. Another five or six passably.' I decided to let him think what he wanted about where I was from.

'That will be useful. You know, I intend to make you work like a dog for the miserable pittance they pay you. Translating, transcribing, copying, trips to the library. That sort of thing. I hope you're up to the task.'

'I'm ready, sir.'

He aimed a stubby finger at me. 'You know, if you call me sir one more time I'm going to come over this desk and throttle you with my bare hands.'

'What would you like me to call you, sir?'

'My name is Irving. If you don't like that, then don't call me anything.'

I nodded.

'Where are you living?'

'Uh, well, I only arrived last night. I'm staying at a motel.'

'That won't do. You'll come and live with me.'

'Sir?'

'What did I say?'

'Sorry. But –'

'It's a matter of convenience. You'll have a room of your own and access to things of mine you'll need.'

'I had planned to start looking for an apartment today.'

'Now you don't have to.'

'But I like my privacy, sir. A space of my own.'

'No problem there. I'll give you all the space you want.'

'I don't know –'

'Look, it's not far, if that's what's bothering you. Walking distance. Well, you could walk it. I can't.'

I didn't know what to say. I was not completely opposed to the idea. But I needed time to think.

'And anyway, you're not going to find anything this time of year. It's the middle of term! Dammit, don't they tell you people anything? Fresh off the boat. Hasn't a clue. What's your name?'

'Kostandin. Kostandin Bitri.'

He grimaced and waved his hand, as if this were just too much.

'How can I be expected to remember that? Look, you like the name Tom, don't you? It's snappy, got a certain ring to it. Think of all the famous Toms there've been: Tom Jefferson. Tom Hardy. Tom Brokaw. You call me Irving. I'll call you Tom. At least for now. We can work out the details later.'

'I guess –'

'Then it's settled. Right now I'm busy, so I'll give you the afternoon. Go back to your motel or whatever it is and get your things. Take them to my house and make yourself comfortable.'

'I don't know where you live, sir.'

He shook his head and scowled. I could only assume he was enjoying himself immensely.

'My jacket's hanging on the back of the door there. Get it, will you?'

I retrieved the jacket, a rumpled grey windbreaker, and handed it to him across the desk.

He pulled a set of keys from the pocket and held them up.

'Key to my house. Key to my car. The car's parked in that big lot just out there.' He turned and waved in the general direction of the window. 'A gold Orion with a sunroof. If you can't find it just press this little button on the doohickey and the horn will beep, or this other button to open the trunk.'

He held the keys out and dropped them into my hand.

'I still don't know where you live.'

'I'm getting to that.'

He tore a sheet from a notepad and started to write.

'You know, my life is an open book. This is a college campus. Don't expect to keep any secrets around here. Darlene will tell you whatever you need to know. All you have to do is ask.'

He handed over the piece of paper. On it were written an address and some sketchy directions.

'I'm placing my trust in you, Tom. I may seem like an eccentric old fool, but I know exactly what I'm doing.' He held out the jacket. 'Hang this up, will you?'

I did what he asked.

'I'll expect to see you back here at five o'clock. Park the car and come up.'

'Thank you,' I said.

'Not at all,' he said. 'I help you, you help me. What could be fairer than that?'

I moved into Spelmann's house and took up residence on the second floor. Though he suffered from muscular dystrophy he lived alone, and from Darlene I learned that his wife had left him ten years ago and his three children had moved away and had very little contact with him. The central staircase was steep, and one concession he had made to his weakened condition was to convert the den on the main floor into a bedroom. My room was large and full of light, and had a full bath and walk-in closet. It was obviously the master suite.

The house was old and cavernous and not, as I had expected given the state of his office, musty and dusty and crammed to the ceiling with books, papers and other paraphernalia of academic life. On the contrary, it was exquisitely appointed. Every piece of furniture looked like something for which an antique dealer could claim an impressive pedigree. Both living and dining room were home to several display cabinets crowded with curios that to my untutored eye appeared antique and beyond value. His music collection filled an entire room of its own and consisted of recordings in every conceivable genre and format (LP, 45, 78, CD) in such ravishing abundance that I could not imagine how he decided what to listen to at any single time. In his study, a cabinet with glass doors contained signed first editions of famous American writers (Hawthorne, James, Thoreau, Hemingway, Twain). There were coins, maps, paintings, sculptures. There was hardly a room or hallway without gleaming hardwood floors protected by some variety of hand-woven Turkish or Oriental carpet. But when I exclaimed over the treasures on display and asked how he had managed to bring it all together under one roof, his only response was a dismissive shrug and the comment, 'I'm a collector.'

Every two weeks a squad of uniformed men and women arrived from a maid service armed with mops and polishers, dusters and vacuums, and spent an entire afternoon in an intensive clean-up operation.

We quickly came to an arrangement. As I had hoped, my duties and responsibilities were confined to assisting his research activities. He was writing a book on passive groups, social aggression and the mob mentality – 'It will be my twentieth,' he informed me over coffee one afternoon – and I was to track down references and obtain the books and articles he needed from the library.

We did our own cooking. On only two occasions – Thanksgiving and New Year's – did we share a meal that had been prepared in his kitchen. Over the holiday we stayed in the house, together but separate, pursuing our own private activities. The only social obligation was dinner on Christmas Day. He had been invited to the home of a colleague from the sociology department, and he made it clear that though I was welcome, no one would count it against me should I choose not to go.

His demands on me were steady but not unreasonable. After Christmas I enrolled in two classes taught by other members of the department, one on 'The Eternal Immigrant', the other on 'The 20th-Century Diaspora', and had plenty of time for my own research. He allowed me the run of the house and free access to everything in it, and insisted that this was part of my remuneration – though of course I knew it was not. His car was available to me whenever it was not in use. The day after I moved in, a laptop computer appeared on the desk in my room, and shortly thereafter he had a wireless network installed in the house. But apart from work, our paths rarely crossed. He made few inquiries into how I was spending my time and seemed to expect that I was amusing myself during my leisure hours. As long as the tasks he assigned to me were completed on schedule, he did not seem interested in what I was up to.

This degree of freedom I found very nearly intoxicating. When I dragged myself to bed each night at two or three in the morning, I lay down giddy with apprehension that I would wake up back in the orphanage or in one of countless apartments I had occupied – tiny and sweltering – while existing on subsistence wages and waiting as various officials assessed a string of applications I had made for overseas employment.

One evening in January we found ourselves together in the living room, sharing a bottle of tawny port that had been a gift from a previous student. The snowstorm raging outside was expected to last through the night. A notice had been circulated that the university would be closed the following day.

The wind howled, but Glenn Gould's recording of the Goldberg Variations was still audible. Spelmann tottered around on his crutches, restlessly regarding and touching things, exuding a strange sort of negative energy. In circumstances such as these, when venturing outside was an option for none but the reckless or foolhardy, he reminded me of a caged beast. The scowl he had worn as a mask at our first encounter was for real tonight, and I wondered if it was this sort of behaviour that had compelled his family to flee his sphere of influence and make lives for themselves in faraway places. (I imagined a hasty late-night exodus down a back staircase while elsewhere in the house he paced and fumed.) Earlier I had watched him pull the record from the shelf and carry it over to the stereo. Balanced on his crutches and his withered legs, he had tipped the record out of its sleeve into his other hand and in a single fluid motion placed it on the turntable, slipped the arm out of its cradle, and set the needle on the rotating disc. But though it was a sort of precision ballet, his every gesture declared frustration with material things that had to be carried from one place to another and fussed over and cared for, and that would not do his bidding simply because he wanted them to.

I had long since gotten over my initial qualms concerning his disability. The crutches had been apparent during our first meeting, and after learning of some recent events in his life I had been suspicious that he was looking for a nursemaid, someone to stand in for his absent family, someone who would fetch things and bring him breakfast in bed. But my misgivings were unwarranted. He was all business and on this occasion seemed disappointed that the next day was going to be, as he put it, 'wasted on frivolities'.

'What do you mean?' I asked, taking a sip of port, which was fruity and sweet but not cloying.

'Snow turns reasonable people into idiots,' he said with evident distaste. He swivelled on the crutches and approached where I sat. 'It's embarrassing. Mark my words, nothing will get done.'

'Are you talking about me?'

'No, Tom. No, no,' he said, shaking his head, standing over me. 'You know what I mean. Don't be deliberately obtuse. I have no doubt you've observed this phenomenon yourself. They have snow where you come from, don't they?'

I thought for a few seconds that his question was rhetorical. But he seemed to actually want an answer.

'Yes,' I said.

'Well,' he declared almost belligerently, 'Surely then you can verify my thesis, that a heavy snowfall – or any snowfall where it is rare – becomes an excuse for adults to behave like children.'

'Perhaps,' I admitted, wondering why he insisted on labouring such a trivial point. 'But it doesn't last. The novelty wears off and people go back to work. Things get done. I don't think you have to worry.'

He grunted and shut his eyes. It almost seemed that what I'd said caused him physical pain.

'Tom, you have to free your mind. You're too literal. It must be your upbringing – they put you in a mental straitjacket early, didn't they. Wouldn't let you think for yourself. Fed you all that Commie bullshit until it was coming out your ears. A steady diet of paranoid psychobabble until you couldn't trust your own mother –'

Our eyes met. More confused than angered, I was about to speak when he seemed suddenly to stoop or sag, as if beneath the weight of some great resentment. Outside, the wind pummelled the front of the house. The structure's beams shifted and groaned. He turned and hobbled away.

'I'm sorry. You didn't deserve that.'

The music had ended. He disappeared into the other room to flip the record over. When he returned he grabbed the bottle from the bar and hurried across the room to refill my glass.

'Snow is a metaphor,' he said, filling his own glass as well, which he then placed on a table and ignored. 'It's the disruption of routine that interests me. The collapse of tradition. Or, more broadly, how novelty affects behaviour. I'm not sure novelty is the right word. But think how under certain conditions a group of people behave one way; under other conditions the same people behave another way. I want to know if this is something we can measure. Can we generalize? Is it quantifiable? Take Nazi Germany, for instance. When those degenerates took power, it acted as a trigger in the general population. People who all their lives had never hurt a fly were suddenly murdering all the Jews, Gypsies and homosexuals they could get their hands on. Blood everywhere and nobody so much as flinched. It's what I want to call the snowfall effect. Because of a change of circumstance they felt free to express decades of repressed emotion in a very short time. It was concentrated and pernicious – what we now think of as evil: an explosion of pent-up hostility that led to an orgasm of violence. And then of course once it got going no one could bring it under control. It's the whole mob thing too. Just think of your own case. The Communists kept a lid on nationalist fervour for fifty years, but when they left town and the lid blew, all that hatred boiled over. When people see snow they feel free to behave like children. It's the same thing.'

'I don't think you can generalize,' I said. I still wasn't sure where this was going. He was agitated and his reasoning seemed off. I attributed this to the storm, and perhaps the alcohol. 'Not all people will behave the same way when circumstances change. Lots of Germans tried to help the Jews. It's not automatic. Most individuals behave according to a moral code. This doesn't go away just because the wind changes direction.'

He nodded. For a minute or two he continued to roam the length of the room, pausing here and there to caress a figurine or touch a painting whenever the wind rose to a gale. During a particularly strong gust I felt the whole house shudder.

'That's good,' he said. 'Another weather metaphor – the wind changes. Sometimes, though, moral standards suffer a general decline. Then it doesn't take much for some depraved buffoon to get into power. Think of Idi Amin.' He glanced at me. 'Obviously I'm feeling my way around these ideas. It's still like I'm on the outside looking in.'

He slid his arms out of the braces and, finally, sat down – and I realized how anxious he had been making me with his fidgeting because I immediately began breathing more easily.

He propped the crutches against the chair. With a noisily expelled breath, he drew his hand across his face.

'I must be losing my mind. Get that for me, will you?'

I retrieved his glass and put it into his outstretched hand.

'Now I'm going to tell you something.' He sipped his port and turned toward me, frowning. 'This is going to be my last book. I'll finish it. I'm not as young as I used to be, but it shouldn't take long. After that I'm going on a trip to Florida to visit my sister. I might stay for a while. She has two sons, both like me.' He slapped his leg. 'I got this later on, in my fifties. They were born with it. What can I say? Faulty genes.'

He must have seen confusion flit across my face.

'The reason I'm saying this, Tom, is that I assume you are going on into a postgraduate program, and while you're doing it you can stay here. Rent free. No strings. I just need someone to watch the place. You'll be doing me a favour.'

I sat up. 'I couldn't –'

'Of course you can. You'd be an idiot not to. Believe me, finding decent accommodations will be your biggest challenge. Everyone knows graduate students have no money but that doesn't stop them from making you pay through the nose for one room the size of a closet with a bunk bed and a piss pot. My first apartment –'

He was interrupted by a blast of wind that buffeted the house and rattled the windows in their frames. It grumbled and howled and grew stronger and shook the dwelling's beams and timbers until I thought for sure the structure would fail, and then grew stronger still. Icy outdoor air swirled into the room and enveloped us, and still the wind grew in strength, swelling like something gone insane. I could almost feel the house bracing itself against the onslaught. I drained the last of my port and shivered. I started counting: sixty, one hundred. I lost count and waited.

Then it was over. The wind gradually slackened and for a few moments the world fell silent. Shortly, out of the silence, came the braying whine of car tires spinning on ice, and, farther in the distance, a siren. Then this faded and, as if it had been there since the beginning of time, the only sound to be heard was Glenn Gould playing Bach.

'Well,' Spelmann said, lowering his eyes, 'we won't go into that. Suffice it to say that I'm not going to live forever and I have to take this trip while I can before the vultures start circling.'

He spoke with a robust voice but when he lifted the glass to his lips his hand was trembling. Soon after this he went to bed.

Our arrangement did not alter. But it was a difficult winter and I sensed he was feeling the strain of his disability to a greater degree than usual. On several mornings I heard him on the telephone with Darlene, and when I was finished working at the campus in the afternoon I would pick up a package or envelope from the office and deliver it to him at the house, which he had not left all day.

The weather was often severe, with storm following storm in quick succession up the coast. We had hardly cleaned up after the last one before the next was upon us. Spelmann had hired a landscaping business to clear the snow from the driveway and sidewalks, but they were so overtaxed that they often did not get to us until so late in the afternoon it seemed pointless for them to do anything. There were other days when the temperature rose so that the snow turned to slush, and then it rained. With the weather in a turmoil Spelmann's caged-beast routine became more frequent. He did not confine himself to the house completely, but sometimes I wished he would. His crutches did not permit him any traction, and the contortions he went through putting on winter boots hardly seemed worth the effort. Occasionally I picked up groceries for him, but he would not let me help him with anything physical. He became ferocious if I showed up at the front door to let him in or, on those occasions when we were coming home together, if I seemed to be hovering about keeping an eye on him. One evening we had gotten out of the car and were approaching the house along the walkway when his footing gave and he tumbled into a snowbank. He let me take his briefcase but at the same time said, 'If you so much as touch me, Tom, by God I'll see that your student visa is revoked and you're on the first boat back to whatever fascist hellhole you came from.' I left him there and went inside. The third time I looked out the window to make sure he was still moving, I caught his furious glare. Immediately I retreated to my room and huddled motionless over a book. It was another half an hour before I heard the door open and sounds of him clattering around in the vestibule.

He seemed calmer after the cycle of storms broke and he began once again to divide his time between campus and home. He worked late into the night, and I watched the stack of clean typed pages on his desk grow. As he neared completion of the project, my role was reduced to fact-checking and verification, and days went by without him asking me to do anything. In the meantime I was accepted into the Ph.D. program for the upcoming fall term. Spelmann had written a glowing letter of recommendation in support of my application.

I arrived home late one evening in March. I was working on a final paper for the Diaspora course and was having trouble with English idioms and the fact that a key paper the professor had suggested I use had been published in Portuguese but, so far as I could tell, had never been translated into a language I could read. My mind was occupied by these issues when I entered the house and I didn't even think about Spelmann and where he might be. It was after midnight when I ventured downstairs to the kitchen, where I intended to make a pot of coffee, hoping it would get me through to the early morning. As I was measuring the grounds I thought I heard something, and then it occurred to me that Spelmann was probably still at work and might want coffee too. I went looking, but he was not in the study, though the light was on and evidence of his recent presence was spread about on the desk and table.

I had never been in his bedroom, but I went into the hall and noticed the door was ajar and this light was also on. Suddenly the absolute stillness that had made my hours here so productive seemed eerily out of place. It seemed to grip the house and everything in it like a kind of fear. I pushed the door open without hesitation. Spelmann lay on the carpet beside the bed, his hands wrapped around the crutches as if he had simply fallen straight over from an upright position. His face was turned so I could see it. His eyes were closed and he looked at peace. I could tell he was dead. He lay completely still and his body rested open and exposed in a manner he would have never tolerated in life. Nevertheless, I went to him and felt for a pulse. There was none. He was cold, but not stone cold, if there's a difference. And I wondered how long he had been lying there and if he'd been dead when I arrived home. There was no way for me to tell.

I did the only thing I could do and phoned for an ambulance. I didn't want him to be alone so I stayed in the bedroom while I waited. I was more stunned than sad. Despite his infirmity he had been a vital force who seemed to fill whatever room he occupied with a peculiar brand of manic intellectual energy. It was beyond comprehension that he could be silenced with such abrupt finality before he had completed his work.

In a short while a couple of paramedics arrived. They loaded him onto a gurney and took him away.

Though I was really nothing more than an employee and had known Spelmann for less than six months, people seemed to think it appropriate to offer me their condolences as if I had lost a loved one. I suppose it was their way of dealing with the shock, and I played the part, shaking hands and accepting well-intentioned assurances that everything would work out and that I had nothing to worry about.

But I won't deny that I was worried and at a loss over what I should do next. A future that had recently appeared stable and secure was now in doubt. There was a degree of uncertainty over the status of my funding, which had been granted through a special international program for undergraduates coming to America for the first time. No one could provide a guarantee that it would not be cut off, and my inquiries ended with a voice mail left on the answering machine of some bureaucrat whose office was in a city I had never heard of. Certainly I would have to look for another place to live. However, given the circumstances, I hesitated to simply unload my problems on someone else. I mentioned my concerns to Darlene, but she was busy and distracted and told me that I should give myself time to recover and not to be too hasty in making my next move. 'There's no hurry,' she said. 'People will understand if you don't want to commit yourself to anything right away.' And so I decided it would be best if, for the moment, I stayed where I was.

Spelmann had not been religious, and with no next of kin close by, the task of making arrangements fell to Heinlein, the department chair – an elderly Austrian with a heavy accent and a deferential manner. Heinlein came to the house a number of times looking for documents, once accompanied by a man in a suit, whom I took to be a lawyer. I was not consulted about anything and did not want to be. I attended the last of my classes, and at home, except to use the kitchen and the laundry, I confined myself to my room. I did not go near Spelmann's office at the department or into his study at the house, and I didn't touch any of his things. When Heinlein visited I stayed out of the way.

At the end of the week when no service or ceremony had been announced, I asked Darlene what was going on.

'Oh, it's the family,' she said. 'None of them live around here and we have to contact them before we can do anything.' She rolled her eyes and I understood that something unforeseen was causing a delay. 'It's going to take a while.'

'I can't stay in that house,' I said. It just slipped out. I hadn't intended to say any such thing. But after the words were spoken, I understood that it was true.

'You're still living there. Oh, my God, that's right.'

It had come to me that I hadn't been sleeping well, and the reason was not that I had found Spelmann dead on the floor, but because with him gone I was, de facto, the custodian of thousands of dollars worth of antiques and collectables that now belonged to someone else. It gave me a headache just thinking about it. I wanted out – the sooner the better.

'No, please, I don't expect you to do anything,' I said, because she had wrinkled her brow and begun shuffling papers back and forth. 'I'll find a place. But when I move out I have to get rid of the keys.'

'Give them to Dr Heinlein.'

'I'll do that,' I said. We both smiled, and I left to begin my search for a new home.

I signed a lease, but the apartment wouldn't be vacant for another month. A week later Heinlein showed up in the middle of the afternoon. With him was a woman. I heard them come in. Immediately the woman's voice rose to such a pitch it set my pulse racing. She seemed to be berating the poor man over something, but I couldn't tell what. I went to the window. Heinlein's car was parked in the driveway behind Spelmann's. The trunk was open and three large black suitcases sat beside it.

There was a slow heavy tread on the stairs. Heinlein tapped on the door and poked his head into the room.

'I'm sorry, Kostandin, but you'll have to get your things out of here. She doesn't mind you being in the house, but she wants this room for herself. She said you can stay in the small bedroom at the end of the hall.'

'Is that the ex-wife?'

He glanced unnecessarily over his shoulder and, approaching me, lowered his voice.

'She claims it was only a separation. According to her, they were still married.' He shrugged. 'It's all the same to me. I'll leave it up to the executor to sort it out. But it means I'm in no position to deny her anything.' He raised his eyebrows.

'No problem,' I said. 'I'll set up in the other room.'

'Good.' He nodded vigorously. 'I'm sorry about this.'

I took my clothes from the closet and gathered my other things and carried everything down the hall into a smaller bedroom, where I laid it all on the bed. Downstairs, the woman's voice remained loud, rising and then fading as her explorations took her from one room to another. When I heard Heinlein leaving no more than five minutes later, I understood that my quiet studious life had come to an end.

The day she arrived I explained to Dolores, Spelmann's widow, about the apartment I had rented and made sure she understood I would soon be leaving. 'Don't hurry on my account,' she said with a broad smile, but there was a hint of sarcasm in her manner that implied the opposite. From then on I spent most of my time at the campus.

Dolores filled the house with cigarette smoke and an intrusive, prob-ing – I am tempted to say nagging – presence. She was a squat, plump woman whose dark golden hair suited her bronzed skin tones. She was not unattractive and appeared many years younger than her hus-band, but I was making her acquaintance at a time of crisis in her life and wearied quickly of her pushy and abrasive manner.

She referred to me as 'the student'. Sometimes I overheard her speaking on the telephone. 'The student is making his escape,' I heard as I was leaving through the front door. And, 'That must be the stu-dent. He comes and goes at all hours,' as I was getting in late one evening.

She conducted herself, speaking loudly on the phone and watch-ing television with the sound turned up, as if unaware that I was in the house, but I think this was pretence because I'm sure very little escaped her notice. Other than a few bland pleasantries we did not speak much, but I had no wish to offend her. Sometimes I asked how her day had gone, and occasionally she addressed similarly meaning-less questions to me. A few times she took a seat in the kitchen when I was there and, with a big smile, asked questions about my accent or where I came from that under different circumstances might have led to a lengthy conversation. I tried to be sociable, but, though she seemed to be making an effort, there was something about her that made me uneasy. I fell into the habit of actively avoiding her whenever I was in the house.

I came down from my room one night. I was working on my last assignment and needed a break. Dolores was seated in the living room wearing a red quilted housecoat. There was an almost-empty glass on the table beside her. She held a cigarette in one hand and a paperback book in the other. I went into the kitchen.

'Tom!' I heard as I was filling the kettle to make a cup of tea. I had told her to call me this after her single bungled attempt to pronounce my real name.

'Yes?'

'We have to talk,' she said when I entered the room. She spoke with some force, though I didn't think she was angry.

'We can talk.'

'Heart to heart,' she said and then embarked upon a slow-motion pantomime of laughter. She tilted her head back, opened her mouth wide, and slapped her knee. At the end of all this, when she finally made a sound, it was the closest thing to a cackle I'd ever heard.

'What I mean is, no more pussyfooting around. We need everything on the table.'

'I agree,' I said. By this time I'd forgotten about making tea. I sat across from her.

'What I need to know is, what did Irving promise you?'

'Promise?' I watched as she tipped the glass up to her mouth. When she returned her attention to me her expression seemed to shift between a smile and a scowl without any actual movement of her facial muscles. 'I don't think I understand,' I said.

'Well, what sort of arrangement did you have with my husband that required you to live in this house?'

'I was helping him with his research.'

She looked at me as if expecting me to go on.

'That's it? Nothing custodial?'

'Pardon?'

'You weren't cooking or cleaning or doing repairs for him? Taking out the garbage?'

'Well, occasionally. All of those things.'

'But he wasn't letting you live here in exchange for services of some kind. Like cleaning, fixing meals. It wasn't contractual, is what I'm getting at.'

'No,' I said. 'I was his research assistant.'

'Well, you seem to have the best of both worlds.'

'What?'

She smiled. 'In case you haven't noticed, my husband isn't doing much research these days.'

I looked at her. She seemed to be having difficulty suppressing her mirth.

'I've already explained I've got another place. I just can't move in yet.'

'But right now you're collecting a bursary from the university and living here. How much rent were you paying?'

'He didn't ask for rent.'

She nodded and drew on the cigarette. I could tell her questions were rhetorical. She already had the answers.

'Poor Irving. He wasn't a practical man. All sorts of charity cases wandered in and out of his life. He gave things away. He was proud of his collections but a lot of this stuff came from his family. His father was the real collector. A connoisseur. While we were together I regarded it as one of my wifely duties to make sure he didn't get taken by some scam artist. It's too bad he was impossible to live with because when I look around now I can see that some of my favourite pieces are missing.'

She stared at me and puffed on the cigarette until there was almost nothing left. Then she stubbed it out. Her expression narrowed.

'What? You think I took something?'

'You or someone else.'

I stood.

'That's crazy. I don't –'

'Oh, sit down.' When I didn't immediately obey she leaned forward and pointed at the chair. 'Sit. Down.'

I resumed my seat. I didn't know what to think but couldn't help wondering how far she was prepared to take this.

'My children will be arriving in the next day or so. There are three of them. My daughter is bringing her children. I'm not telling them they have to stay in a hotel when this house is basically empty.'

'You want me to get out. I can get out.'

'I want,' she said with emphasis, 'you to earn your keep.' She tilted her head and smiled. 'I think it's only fair.' She said this in a chirpy voice as she set about lighting another cigarette.

I was annoyed but also uneasy. I would be out of here soon enough, but I could see that letting me stay was an act of pure charity for which I should be grateful. The only other thought that came to me was that I had nothing to bargain with.

'I didn't steal anything,' I said weakly.

'I didn't say you did.'

She wouldn't take her eyes off me. For a moment I suffered the horrific sensation of what it must feel like to be a bug in a jar, watching your tormentors making plans for your demise. But I had no standing. I could not protest or argue, because she was right. The house and everything in it were hers. I did not belong here. And yet I found repugnant the notion that she would accuse me of theft and see me punished if I refused to cooperate.

'What do I have to do?'

She gave me, as she put it, a choice. I could pay her five hundred dollars a month rent retroactive to the day Spelmann had died, when I stopped being a research assistant and started being, in her words, a 'freeloader'. Or I could let her hire me to do the household chores, in exchange for which I could stay in the room that Spelmann had occupied.

'You can cancel your lease on the other place. I'm sure they won't mind. Just tell them you've got an offer that only an idiot would turn down.' She smiled magnificently as she stubbed out the half-smoked cigarette. 'But I won't ask you to decide this minute. I can be generous. Stay the night. Get some sleep. Tell me in the morning.'

She sipped her drink and turned the smile on me again. And I could see how in her youth she would have used that smile in combination with other physical attributes to disarm and captivate even the most cerebral of men. Maybe she had been a student of Spelmann's and fixed her sights on him as a likely mate, possibly after listening to him boast about the family's history and importance. I could see her running to the library to look up names and designations that Spelmann would have used without thinking that would have meant nothing to her, as they had to me when I first arrived here: Brancusi, the Ardabil Carpet, Maurice Utrillo, Spode creamware.

'What if I just leave?' I suggested. 'Tonight. Now.'

She shrugged.

'Try it and we'll see what happens.'

The situation was, of course, intolerable.

'Thank you,' I said, and went upstairs to my room.

In a few minutes my bag was packed. I waited until she had gone to bed before creeping back downstairs. I left the key on the hall table and made sure the door was locked when I pulled it shut behind me. I took only those items I had brought with me when I arrived. The laptop, a sweater and some books that Spelmann had given me, pens I'd found in the desk where I'd done most of my work, I left behind. It was a cool night, and cloudy. Possibly it would rain. But I felt no need to hurry because I had nowhere to go. I just kept walking.

The first thing I saw when I awoke was the nurse's face, only inches above mine. She was young and her dark hair was gathered tightly beneath a cap. I saw her for only a second before she was gone.

The left side of my head throbbed. I tried to lift my arm, but it was weighted down. There was terrible pain throughout my body. I groaned and lost consciousness.

I awoke again. I didn't know how much time had passed. I was lying in a bed beneath a white ceiling. There was light behind me, but I couldn't move my head to locate its source. I fought the pain, which seemed to fill my body like liquid filling a vessel. After a few moments I recognized that it was more severe in my left leg and arm, and in my head, than elsewhere. The next thing I noticed was that the left side of my head was bandaged. The bandages covered my eye. I could not seem to move any of my limbs. The room stank. Food odours mingled with the stench of disinfectant. I tried to cry out.

I must have lost consciousness again because I seemed to awaken. Someone was aiming a penlight into my eye. He withdrew it and dropped it into the pocket of his lab coat.

'You're a lucky man,' he said while he jotted something on a paper attached to a clipboard. 'There's no brain damage. You won't lose your eye. And you have no broken bones. There's no reason why you should not be up and about in a week or two.'

Even though he was standing still, he wavered in and out of focus. He was thin and seemed to be young. He wore a tie and there was a stethoscope draped around his neck.

'What happened?' I asked. As I spoke a new pain shot up the side of my face. My voice sounded strange and garbled, as if I were trying to talk through a mouthful of food.

'The trauma will have affected your memory. You were brought in a week ago. At that point we didn't know if you were going to live. But your improvement has been very encouraging. Now that you're conscious I have no doubt you'll make a full recovery. There will be some scarring.'

I was going to nod but the pain in my head stopped me.

He placed his hands on my neck at the base of my jaw and gently swivelled my head from side to side.

'Mobility is good,' he remarked, as if to another person I couldn't see. Then he was gone.

I slept.

I was eating my first meal of solid food. Pureéd chicken, mushy peas, green Jell-o and pale tea. A tube running from a bag of clear liquid suspended from a pole was attached to my right arm. I had not yet left the bed, but a physiotherapist had come and examined my injured arm and leg, and told me it would be at least a couple of days before I could stand unaided. I was disappointed to learn I had to wait that long because the catheter was very uncomfortable. But this was nothing compared to the pain I suffered all through the left side of my body. My headaches came on so suddenly and were so violent that they inserted a needle into my drip that fed another medicine into my bloodstream, a medicine so strong it carried me off into a world of swirling dream visions.

When the woman came to collect my tray I said, 'I can chew, you know. Maybe you could tell them I'm not sucking everything through a straw.'

Businesslike, she took the tray and fed it into a slot in her cart. She glanced at me but didn't say anything.

I shared a room with three other patients. The walls were bare and the lighting harsh, but it didn't matter because the curtains around our beds were drawn most of the time. I had glimpsed the old man in the bed next to mine, who, with his collapsed features and skin yellowed like old newspaper, seemed on the verge of death. I couldn't hear him breathe. I only knew he was alive because he mumbled in his sleep. As far as I had seen, the others, like me, had not had any visitors.

Sometimes I felt as if I'd been put in a ward for hopeless cases. I enjoyed it when the nurses came in. They were always making jokes and trying to sound cheerful. Except for the meal-cart lady, the hospital workers were friendly and talkative.

I awoke from a doze one afternoon to see a policeman sitting in the chair next to my bed. A nurse was with him, but the moment she saw I was awake she smiled at both of us and left.

He stood and held out his hand. He was broad-shouldered and bulky with a shaved head and a thick neck. 'Constable Serge Druon,' he said. When we shook, his grip was too strong. I gasped at the pain.

'Oh, sorry,' he said. He withdrew his hand and then appeared unsure what to do next.

'I'm all right.' I flexed my fingers to show him he had not hurt me. 'You have some questions?'

He cleared his throat and flipped open a notebook. 'The night you were brought in. The twenty-third.' He looked at me.

'I suppose,' I said. 'I don't remember.'

'It says here you were brought in on the twenty-third.'

'I'm not questioning that,' I said. 'I just can't tell you if you're right or wrong.'

He looked puzzled and stared at me for a few seconds longer than seemed necessary.

'Regarding the night of the twenty-third then,' he went on finally. 'What can you tell me about that night?'

'I don't remember that night,' I said.

He looked at me as if he didn't believe me. 'You don't recall anything?'

'No,' I said. 'I've gone over it a hundred times, but the last thing I remember is talking to someone from one of my classes. Class was finished and we were walking out. His name is Robert. Then the next thing I remember is waking up here.'

After writing down what I'd said he asked, 'Did you go anywhere with this Robert after your class?'

'No. I don't know him very well. We're only in one class together. I've never seen him outside of class.'

He nodded as he wrote. 'What time did this class end?'

'About five-thirty.'

'And what do you do after this class, under normal conditions?'

'Depending how I feel, I sometimes go straight home, or to the library to study, or to the Student Union for a beer.'

'Did you go to the Student Union for a beer on the night of the twenty-third?'

'I don't know,' I said. 'I can't remember.'

His face betrayed no reaction. He flipped over the page in the notebook and studied what was written there. 'The university is downtown, in the centre of the city.'

'Yes.'

'You specialize in –' he paused. 'Indo-European languages.'

'Yes, that's right.'

'You live in the Anglewood apartment building on Renfrew Street?'

'Yes.'

'You were found at the corner of Wilson and Firth in the north end of the city.'

He looked at me, possibly for confirmation.

'I'll have to take your word for it.'

'It says here that at approximately 2:45 a.m. a vehicle operated by a Mr Joseph Ottway pulled to the side of Firth Street near Wilson. Mr Ottway stated he noticed something on the sidewalk that looked like a pile of garbage or a bundle of clothes. When he pulled over he saw it was a body and immediately called the emergency number.'

He glanced at me before continuing.

'The body was that of a Caucasian male, late twenties. The injuries were consistent with being struck by a vehicle: lacerations and extensive bruising to the left side of the body. Significant loss of blood from a head wound. The individual was stabilized at the scene and brought to the trauma unit at 3:15 a.m.'

'So it looks like I was hit by a car.'

'Looks like it,' he said. 'Do you have any idea how you got to the corner of Wilson and Firth?'

'None?'

'Do you know why you would be in that part of the city? Do you frequent any clubs or know anybody who lives there?'

I shook my head. 'No.'

'This Robert from your class doesn't live there?'

'I have no idea where he lives.'

'Have you ever had any dealings with Joseph Ottway?'

'No.'

He leafed through a few more pages of the notebook.

'Did you have significant amounts of money with you that night?'

'No.'

'You weren't going somewhere to buy drugs? There are known drug dealers who operate in the neighbourhood around Wilson and Firth. It's notorious, actually.'

'I don't do that sort of thing.'

He nodded and studied the notebook again.

'Do you have a girlfriend?'

'No.'

He leafed slowly through the final few pages of the notebook before flipping it shut.

'Our investigation will be kept open, but I doubt we'll find who did this.' He picked up his cap, which I now noticed had been resting on the bed at my feet. 'We suspect the attack was random or the person was drunk. You were crossing the street and someone ran you down. There were no skid marks. It might have been accidental, but because you can't remember what happened our investigation can't really proceed. Random assaults are just about the most difficult crimes to solve because there's no motive. In a case like this witness testimony is crucial, but no witnesses have come forward.'

My face was still bandaged and my vision had grown cloudy, so I could not read his expression. But I got the feeling he wanted more from me than I'd been able to provide.

'I'm sorry,' I said.

He ignored this. 'If you remember anything else you can contact us. Any detail can help. Even if you think it's not important, it could be enough for us to get a fix on what happened.'

'I'll try,' I said.

He nodded and left. We did not shake hands again. I rested my head on the pillow. His questions had exhausted me. In a minute I was asleep.

My face was covered with scrapes and purple with bruises. My eye was still swollen shut. I walked with difficulty, labouring up the hall with the aid of a tubular metal walker and attended by a nurse who pushed my IV pole on wheels. She was the nurse whose face I had seen when I first woke up. Her name was Elizabeth Piper. She kept her hand on my elbow the whole time, as if afraid I might fall. Her concern seemed sincere. Every few minutes she asked if I wanted to stop or if there was anything she could get for me.

'No,' I said. 'There's nothing.'

'Do you have any brothers or sisters?'

'No. I was an only child.'

'What about your parents?'

'They're dead.'

'I'm so sorry.'

'It's nothing to be sorry about. They've been dead for a long time.'

'Do you keep in touch with anyone back home?'

'For a while I wrote letters to friends. But right after I left I was moving around so much that if they wrote back the letters never reached me. Now I've been away for so long I don't know if any of them are still there. I could write again. I still have their addresses.'

'Why were you moving around so much?'

'I had to go where I could find work. Sometimes the jobs I had didn't last very long. Two weeks or a month. It was a couple of years before I was able to get a job that lasted for more than three months. Everywhere I went I was a foreigner. It made things very difficult. You have to be prepared to take jobs that nobody else wants, even if it means packing up and leaving after only a few weeks.'

She shook her head. 'I don't know how people can stand to live like that, always moving from place to place – never having a chance to settle. As soon as you arrive in one place you have to start thinking about leaving to go to the next. It would drive me crazy.'

'My country is very poor and the people have always been forced to leave to find work. Whole families do it. It's like a tradition. It's how we survive. Bulgaria and Greece are our neighbours and a lot of people go there. I spent time in Greece and Serbia and a few other countries before coming over here. When I left home, I knew what was going to happen and I knew how I was going to be treated. I knew I would be expected to work for lower wages because I was foreign. It's not legal, but it's the system. If I complained, they would have me deported. One phone call would be the end of me. So I did twice the work for half the wage and smiled the whole time. Not everyone I worked for was like that. But because I was foreign it took a while to build trust. When I look back it wasn't so bad.'

'It sounds awful.'

'It always sounds worse than it is. I didn't like some of the things I had to do, but I met some wonderful people.'

'Do you ever think about going back?'

'All the time.'

'I'm sorry, I don't mean to be so nosy.'

'I don't mind,' I said. 'Most of my memories are good ones.'

'I'm sorry about what happened to you.'

We walked in silence for a minute.

'Did you live near the water?' she asked. 'I love the ocean.'

'Yes. When I was a child our house wasn't far from a lake that was twenty-five miles long. I remember you could smell the water and hear the birds.'

'It must be beautiful, where you're from.'

'It used to be beautiful,' I said. 'But the government was corrupt and incompetent and there were no regulations. They let lumber companies cut down trees in the national parks, and factories dumped their waste into the lakes and rivers. It got even worse when the Soviet Union collapsed and everyone started fighting everyone else. People did whatever they wanted. It's going to take years for the countryside to recover.'

For a moment she didn't say anything. The phone at the nurse's station rang and someone answered it.

'I've been to Italy.'

'I've never been there,' I said.

'We went to Rome, and then took a bus to Capri. We stopped here and there to visit museums and cathedrals. There were lots of little towns along the way. I remember it rained a lot. But the flowers were lovely.'

I nodded.

'Everywhere we went the children were selling flowers. I had to buy them. I couldn't resist. Everyone was so friendly. But you have to watch out for pickpockets.'

'In my country,' I said, 'the children collect and sell anything they can find. It can mean the difference between eating and starving. The most popular activity is collecting scrap metal, because the dealers will pay a good price for it. Especially shell casings. But the problem is that the children searching for scrap metal sometimes come across unexploded bombs and land mines.'

'That's terrible. Why do their parents let them do it?'

I looked at her. 'The parents have no choice. They depend on the income. You have no idea what it's like. There are no jobs and there's no government assistance. People will do anything to make money because they don't want to starve. In my country when it rains, people get wet.'

Immediately I regretted saying this, because I liked her and I knew she would find these things alarming. She made no further comment and we walked on in silence. My leg was very weak and the pain had crept into my spine, but I made myself walk all the way to the television room.

On our way back I said, 'I think I'd like to get into bed now.'

She helped me into the bed, drew the curtain, and went away. I had grown drowsy and when I closed my eyes I saw myself getting into the back of a taxi. It was night. I was not alone. The person next to me spoke to the driver and told him where we were going. I tried to look at who was with me, but it was like my head was locked in a vice. I couldn't turn.

I thought that if I didn't force my thoughts in that direction, something about why I had gone to the corner of Wilson and Firth Streets would come back to me. But weeks later I still remembered nothing. The last thing I could recall was speaking to Robert while we were leaving class. Everything after that was a blank. I could not even remember what Robert and I had talked about. When the police had asked me what his last name was and how to contact him, I'd had to tell them I didn't know. But I doubted he would be able to provide any useful information because we had never met or socialized outside of class.

One night I awoke while it was still dark. There was wind and I think it was raining. I didn't know why I had woken up until I realized that my head was filled with memories. They had nothing to do with the night I was injured. Instead, my mind had taken me back twenty-five years. I was a child and I was walking down the hallway in a house, the house where I had lived with my parents. I stopped outside the door to a room. The door was closed but not locked. I twisted the doorknob and pushed. Inside, the light was dim, but against the closed curtains I could see the outline of someone lying in a bed. I seemed to have no fear. I went closer. The person in the bed was murmuring or moaning, and I knew without thinking about it that it was my grandmother and that she was dying. I understood in a childish way that she would soon be going on a long journey all by herself, and even though I was sad about this I had been told that I would see her again some day. Now that I was in the room, which had been forbidden to me, I didn't know what to do. I became conscious of a sharp and oily smell that got in my nose and nearly made me sneeze. I decided to examine the things on the dresser, the little bottles and vials that had always seemed so precious and mysterious. I had never been allowed to touch them, but now that Grandmother was going away it would be safe to look at these things. I grabbed a blue crystal bottle and brought it to my nose, removing the decorative stopper as I did this so I could smell the dark liquid. There was no odour. I shook the bottle, but the liquid didn't move and I realized that it had become solid. I was returning the bottle to its place on the dresser when I heard a sound, and I turned to see my grandmother looking at me from the bed. She seemed agitated and was making a sound like a cough or a grunt. She reached out toward me and opened her mouth. I was suddenly scared, because she was not dead yet and she had caught me in her room. Somehow the bottle was on the floor between my feet, smashed. I had not heard a thing. Then my mother was in the doorway, her hands on either side of her head. The room echoed with moaning and wailing.

I didn't know if this was a memory or something my mind had manufactured. True or not, it was vivid and frightening and filled with enough detail to bring back my childish fear of being discovered where I did not belong.

In the days that followed, my childhood returned to me in a series of dreams or visions, complete with the smells and sounds of the house and town where I had spent my earliest years. I concluded that the injury had unlocked something in my head, broken open some conduit to my past and unloosed a torrent of memory, though as each vision unfolded it seemed more than just memory. The people in these dreams lived and breathed. I felt the heat of the sun and the cool of the rain. My father and mother moved and spoke as they had in life. Old people trudged along, leading a goat or a sow to market. When I ventured down a street the dirt and dust got into my hair and my eyes. Each sensation touched me beneath my skin and left a mark.

I recalled a spring day when my father took me with him to a musical showcase at his school, the same school I would attend when I was older. He was a music teacher, and his students were to give a demonstration of their skills. The school was only a single building, whitewashed, crumbling, but he was proud of his position there. He played the violin and we were sometimes treated to evening recitals at home. At the school, he taught whatever instrument the student wanted to play, even if he knew nothing about it. He even taught piano, though the piano at the school had suffered damage from being frequently moved from place to place for use in various events, and he had to tune it himself. We walked to school together that spring day. It was warm and had lately rained. The dirt road had turned to mud and the air was so damp it left a residue on the skin. We entered the schoolroom. He had told me it was his room and that he was the only person allowed to teach there. The children cheered at the sight of him. I never thought students could love their teacher so much. He put me in a chair at the head of the class so I could see everything that was going on. He cleared a space at the front and invited his music students to take their places. Ten students performed that day, four in one group and another six by themselves. While the students played their pieces, I realized that my father must teach subjects other than music. There was a map of the world on the wall and the chalkboard was covered with sums, and sentences with blanks in them. The room smelled of mould and damp. My father smiled all during the recital. He didn't seem to care if the students made mistakes. Since they were not likely to find joy and freedom in other aspects of their lives, he wanted them to experience the joy and freedom of making music. Later, if they kept up with their studies, they could worry about perfection. On the way home he took me to a friend's house for ice cream. Even though it was warm out a fire was blazing in the grate. The house smelled of wool and pine resin and felt dry and cozy. We sat in front of the fire with our ice cream and I listened to my father and his friend tell each other stories. When he laughed, the creases in my father's face disappeared and he seemed very young, hardly old enough to be a teacher in a school. He laughed like someone who hadn't a worry in the world.

I remembered walking in the hills outside of town with my mother and some of her friends, young women like her who were married to farmers or carpenters or whose husbands had left town in search of work. All of the women had brought children and even babies. My mother had packed a basket with our lunch, and at the top of a high hill we sat in the grass and shared the food we had brought. Everyone had brought something different. There was cake and fruit and dried meat sausage and jars of yoghurt with honey, nuts, traditional sweetened bread, cheese, and fresh water from the well. My mother told stories and listened to the stories of her friends. Everyone laughed and not a word was said about the work they were neglecting. I listened for a while and then along with some other boys decided to explore the hill and the surrounding forest. We had finished eating and set off running and yelling. My mother called to me not to go far and to come back in twenty minutes because we would soon be going home. I followed the others, but was easily outpaced because they were all older than me. I remembered the scent that filled the air, a wild musky aroma, medicinal but invigorating. The afternoon was hot, and the sun hung directly overhead in the hazy sky. The field buzzed with the heat. Everything seemed suspended. It was cooler in the forest. The boys organized a war game, naming themselves after the famous generals who fought in the wars and were feared by our enemies. I would be the king, they said, which sounded wonderful because I would tell them what to do. But in real life they told me the king stayed by himself in the palace while the generals went out to defend the country, so I sat on a stump and watched as they took their sticks and set about defending the little patch of cleared territory against imaginary invaders. I soon grew bored with this and left them to their game. Nobody noticed I was gone. I wandered back out to the grassy field, where I saw a raven circling in the sky, high up. I stood and watched him. He was alone. I wondered where his friends were and whether he was flying in circles up in the sky because he was looking for them. I lay down in the grass to watch him, to keep him company, and that was where my mother found me more than a hour later, lying in the grass asleep, keeping a raven company.

The memories came at any time of the day or night. I could be walking in the hall or eating lunch, and a scene from my past would play in my head like a movie. Elizabeth was often present because she was coming in on her days off to be with me, and she grew accustomed to the way I suddenly stopped talking or listening and grew vague and remote, as if my brain had switched itself off. When the memories came they took possession of me. I couldn't do anything to stop them. Afterward, she would ask, 'What was it this time?'

I left the hospital, walking with the help of a cane. The sight had returned to my left eye and the pain was gone, except for headaches that could come upon me so quickly and unexpectedly I always had to have pills with me. Elizabeth brought her car to the hospital and drove me to my apartment, which she had already cleaned because I had let her take the key. I had been so busy recovering from my injuries that I had not thought to ask why she was doing these things for me. At some point during my convalescence I realized that I was seeing her face more often than I should have. It was unimaginable that anyone could work such long hours. But I never questioned her solicitude and was grateful for her constant presence. Without my noticing, we had become friends.

Elizabeth had taken me shopping and we were driving back to the apartment. After less than a year I did not know the city well, and the drive home was taking so much longer than the drive to the mall I thought she might be lost.

'What part of town is this?' I asked. We'd passed a cemetery and some old brick buildings that appeared to be vacant, then an empty parking lot surrounded by a wire fence. Among the garbage strewn on the sidewalk and blowing in the gutter were advertising flyers, fast-food containers, plastic bags, and pop cans. A group of teenagers or young men wearing loose-fitting clothes huddled in a dark knot at a street corner. She stopped at a red light.

'I was wondering if you would find any of this familiar. We're on Firth Street. The next block down is the intersection with Wilson.'

I nodded and glanced around. The cross street where we waited extended as far as I could see. It was lined on both sides with parked cars. The houses were old and run down. The windows of some were covered with plywood.

She smiled at me and took my hand. 'Are you all right?'

'None of this looks familiar,' I said.

The light changed and she resumed driving.

'We can go straight home if you want. I thought it might jog your memory to see where it happened. I hope you don't mind.'

'Were you talking to anyone at the hospital about me?'

'You mean did I ask if I should do this?'

I nodded.

'No. I just thought, since we're out in the car.' She paused. 'I'm sorry. It's a stupid idea.'

'Is this the corner?'

The intersection was just ahead of us. Elizabeth didn't answer. The light turned red and she stopped.

'I'm not angry. I just wasn't expecting it. Can we get out and look around?'

She smiled again, which pleased me because I thought that maybe I'd made her feel bad with my question about the hospital. When the light changed she drove through the intersection and pulled the car over to the curb.

My leg was stiff after sitting, but I was able to lift myself out of the seat before she got around to my side to help me.

'You don't learn, do you?' she laughed. She took my arm as we walked.

I didn't recognize anything. The street, the houses, the busy convenience store with the name Nasmi's above the window in shiny red letters – everything was new to me. Firth Street descended in a lazy incline toward the city and for a few moments we stood at the top of the hill looking down. It was a clear day and from this vantage point we could see how the city sprawled in every direction, as if, lacking both design and reason, it was helpless to stop itself. In the distance stood the majestic high-rise office towers that had so impressed me when I first arrived. Beside these were tall, cantilevered cranes and the skeletons of new construction. It was both monstrous and beautiful.

We crossed the street.

'This is where they found you,' Elizabeth said, indicating a portion of sidewalk beneath some overgrown shrubs that had burst through a low iron fence in front of a small apartment building. The fence was set upon a brick wall, about a foot in height.

'You were lying right here, I think,' she said, looking down and touching a spot close to the wall with her foot.

'You know this for sure?'

'I wanted to see for myself,' she said. 'When they brought you in I could hardly believe how badly off you were. You looked like you'd been through a train wreck. Of course, I'm a nurse, so I did my job and treated the injuries without thinking about how you might have got them. Then the police came and I heard that you'd been found beaten up and left to die. I thought how terrible it was that someone could come to this country and end up hurt so badly and that it was deliberate.'

'But you didn't know anything about me. I might have been out drinking and got into a fight, or tried to cheat some drug dealer. It could have been my fault.'

She shook her head. 'I didn't believe that for a minute.' She looked at me. 'I drove out here because the better I got to know you the more confusing it became. I thought I might find an answer. But when I got here, there was just the yellow police tape and blood all over the sidewalk. There was so much blood.'

'Here?'

I knelt down to examine the spot where Ottway had found me. Elizabeth kept her hand on my shoulder to steady me. I pushed aside the branches of the shrub to get a better look, but there was nothing new to be seen or discovered. The tape was gone and all traces of blood had been washed away.

With the cane I pushed myself up from the kneeling position. Elizabeth took my hand.

'It doesn't really matter now, does it? I mean, what if you had all the answers? It wouldn't change what happened.'

I looked around. From this spot, where I had almost died, I saw nothing that I could recall ever having seen before. None of the people walking by looked familiar. Even the air I was breathing seemed strange. Elizabeth, with her long dark hair trailing down her back, her sweet oval face that reminded me of the peasant girls back home – even she was a stranger. I didn't know anything about her.

We turned and walked back to the car.

I had been placed in the home of a family named Schtetler. There were three boys, all older than me. The father worked at two jobs and was almost never around. The mother was a frantic, watchful woman who was always scrubbing, washing or cooking. I had been told at the state agency where placements were arranged that the family had asked to have me in their home and that I must not make myself a burden to them. I was careful therefore to thank them for every meal and to be polite at all times. I did not want to risk being sent back to the orphanage.

The walk home from school took me along a street lined with concrete apartment buildings that were identical except for a big wooden letter fastened to the wall beside the front entrance of each one. The letters were painted different colours. A was yellow. B was red. C was green. Further along in the alphabet they ran out of colours and had to use the same ones over again. They also ran out of letters so that after building Z (black) the next building was AA (blue). The family I was staying with didn't live in one of these but in a smaller building farther from the school than all the lettered buildings. I had to walk past the entire alphabet in order to get home.

That afternoon I was alone because the teacher had asked me to stay after classes were over. I had been enrolled on the previous day, and she had kept me back to ask me some questions. Where did I come from? Who were my friends? Where was I living? I told her the name of the town where I used to live and said that I didn't have any friends and that I was living with people I knew nothing about. Instead of expressing sympathy, she seemed suspicious and asked the same questions again. I couldn't understand why she didn't believe me. Finally she said I could go, but she followed me into the hallway and watched me walk all the way to the end. I went to my locker and got my things, and I was walking along the street wondering what I had done to make her think I was lying when I heard a man's voice.

'Hello there.'

I stopped and looked back the way I had come, but all I could see were a couple of children taking turns beating on a tin can with a stick, and an old man with a crooked back trying to step from the sidewalk down into the street with the help of a cane. I started walking again but stopped when the voice called out a second time.

'Hello. Over here!'

He shook the chain link fence, which rattled against its posts.

What I saw when I turned was a dwarfish man of slight build, wearing a dark coat that reached to his feet. He gripped the fence with both hands and smiled, revealing two rows of crooked yellow teeth. I did not hesitate to approach him.

'What's your name?'

When I told him he surprised me by saying, 'You're new here, aren't you, Kostandin?'

'Yes.' I looked down because there seemed to be something shameful about this.

To my astonishment he said, 'You're staying with the Schtetlers.'

'How did you know that?'

He regarded me earnestly.

'Pirgi knows everything,' he said and winked.

'Pirgi?' I said. 'Is your name really Pirgi?' I was shocked to hear him say this because the word pirgi means 'little pig.'

He nodded and seemed sad and proud at the same time. Something in his eyes, which were brown and flecked with tiny veins, made me welcome the idea of telling him about myself. It was a feeling that swept over me, like a sudden understanding.

'That's what they call me.' He tilted his head. 'You should come over here so we can talk more easily.'

There was a break in the fence not far from where we were standing and without a second thought I scrambled over to his side. He was only a few inches taller than I was.

'This is where I live,' he declared, and with a broad gesture indicated the ugly apartment building that jutted skyward behind us. Beside the front entrance was the letter P. The letter was a deep shade of violet but some of the paint had flaked off. 'I've been living here for so long I can't remember living anywhere else. I think I was living here before they put up the building.'

'That's impossible,' I said. 'You couldn't be living here if there was no building.'

He seemed to think for a moment and then admitted, 'Perhaps you're right. I was probably living with my mother and father in their house. But I can't remember any of that. I was only a baby.'

While he talked he led me across the lawn and behind a clump of trees to a bench. Next to this was a deserted play area with swings and a slide, both of which were broken. The wooden walls of a sand-box had collapsed and the sand had spilled over the grass. We sat down.

'Do you like it here in our city?'

I didn't know what to say since I had only been there a few days. I shrugged.

'I admit it's not beautiful. But it has some good points. There are the ruins of the old cathedral. And our football team has reached the first circle three years in a row. Someday they'll win the state championship. Where are you from?'

'Elbasan.' This was not true. But since he knew where I was staying without me telling him, I wanted to see what he would say.

'Ah, you're testing me. But you can't fool Pirgi. I know you're from Shkodër.'

'How do you know that?' I asked again. I wondered who could have been talking about me.

'All I do is make conclusions based on the facts,' he said. 'For example, I saw Mrs Schtetler walking with you to the school the other day, probably to register you. She wouldn't be doing that if she had no reason to, not with three boys of her own to worry about. And just now when you spoke I noticed something in your voice that I've heard before. Your accent reminds me of people I know who come from around Lake Scutari. You probably can't tell, because it's the way you speak. But it's there. I knew the name of that town, so I guessed. I'm lucky sometimes too.'

This explanation seemed reasonable enough and my worries were dispelled.

'Now,' he began, 'I want you to tell me something, and be truthful about it. What do you like about our city, and what don't you like?'

I thought for a moment and what came to mind was that you could lose yourself in a city this size. I told him that I could still remember what it was like to live in a small village where everybody knew everybody else by their first name. I didn't like the way everyone seemed to know what you were up to and where to find you. It seemed to me that in a large city it would be easy to slip off somewhere and disappear, if that's what you wanted to do.

Pirgi nodded and for a moment he seemed to ponder what I'd said.

'And why do you suppose someone would want to disappear?'

I shrugged. 'I don't know.'

He stared at me for a long time and I began to feel uncomfortable again. Then he smiled.

'Well, if that's what you like about our city, what is it you don't like?'

I said that I found the people unfriendly. I told him about my teacher, and how she had refused to believe me when I answered her questions. The Schtetlers were the same. So far Mr Schtetler hadn't said a single word to me. All he ever did was look at me, and I could see in his eyes that he didn't trust me. Mrs Schtetler was different because she was nice, but she also seemed on her guard when I was with her, as if she thought she was being watched. The boys ignored me. But so far, all I knew about living in the city was that people were scared of each other and didn't trust anyone, especially a stranger.

'It's the same in every city,' Pirgi said without hesitating, as if this complaint were a familiar one. 'People everywhere are under all kinds of pressure. Food is scarce. Nobody has enough money. You shouldn't let it bother you.'

I nodded. I was going to stand up and leave, but he didn't give me the chance.

'Since we're friends now I am going to tell you something. In a city like this one, most of the people are hard working and honest. They go to their jobs, they follow the rules, and they don't cause any trouble. They live orderly lives and they should be proud, because they are the foundation of our society. But there are others, like Mr Schtetler, who would like nothing better than to disrupt the order that our leaders work so hard to maintain. I know they tell you in school that there are rules and that you have to follow them. That's easy for most of us to understand. But imagine if there were no rules, if you could do whatever you liked. Well, there are people who want our society to be like that. They want to come and go as they please and they don't want to do what they're told. There aren't many of these anarchists, but they're still dangerous because you can't tell who they are just by looking at them. They could be your best friend, or your neighbour, or your brother. It's impossible to tell. So we always have to be looking out. That's why you sometimes find people acting strangely, but it's only because they don't know yet that you're one of the good ones. Once they know they can trust you, you'll be welcome anywhere and treated fairly.'

I nodded. Everything he said made sense.

'It's too bad that some people want to force their views on every-one. It makes life hard for all of us. But what I've found is that if we stick together, no one will be able to hurt us. When we all think the same way and work toward common goals, nothing can stop us. We have to help one another. Are you willing to help?'

'Yes,' I said. Suddenly I wanted nothing more than to be a member of Pirgi's group, working selflessly to make the world a better place and rooting out those who stood in our way. It seemed a noble and decent thing to do and satisfied a craving within me that I hadn't even realized was there. I felt lucky to have crossed paths with this dwarfish man in the long dark coat.

'That's good. I can see that you're a good boy and that you'll grow up to be a good man. What I need from you is this. We believe Mr Schtetler is an anarchist, but we have no proof. We need someone to watch him and write down when he goes out and when he comes home. You don't have to follow him. We just need the times. And let me know if anything unusual happens or if he has any visitors, or even if he and his wife have an argument. It might be that we're wrong about him. In this case your information will help us by clearing him of suspicion. Once we know for sure that he's innocent we can put our resources somewhere else. But if our suspicions are true, then he'll be arrested. I know it sounds bad, but that's only because when we hear that someone has been arrested we think they've been put in jail. However, if Mr Schtetler is arrested he'll be put into a re-education program. It will only last a little while and then he'll be home with his family. Do you think you can do this for me?'

'Yes,' I said.

'Good. You write the information down in a notebook and put the notebook in a safe place. Write everything down carefully and keep it on one page. When the page is filled, tear it out and bring it with you. I won't talk to you for a few days, but I'll be watching. When you have the page with you I want you to signal to me from the street. A wave or a nod will do. We can sit and have another chat and you can give me the page. Above all, don't tell anyone what we've been talking about. There's no need for anyone else to know. Now, I need you to tell me that you understand.'

I nodded. 'I understand.' My heart was racing and I could hardly suppress my smile, but I said this solemnly, as if reciting an oath.

'We'll talk again in a few days. Go home and don't say anything to anyone about this.'

I ran toward the street. When I looked back he was still sitting there watching me. His presence filled me with warmth that radiated from deep inside me. Just knowing he was there made me feel safe. It was as if I'd found my guardian angel. He smiled and waved, and I set off toward the Schtetlers' apartment filled with a sense of mission and importance.

I had a small notebook that I had brought with me from the orphanage, and I used this to make my record of Mr Schtetler's activities. Pirgi had made it sound like a simple task when he explained what he wanted me to do, but I quickly discovered that Mr Schtetler was a man who did not keep to a schedule and who seemed to have no need for sleep. I also felt the need for secrecy like a burden on my shoulders, and took measures to conceal my note-taking from the youngest Schtetler boy, Juré, who was sharing his bedroom with me. Because I could not lock my belongings away, I carried the notebook with me at all times and slept with it under my pillow. I had decided that if anyone asked what I was doing I would say I was writing poetry.

For the first few days I was able to keep records that were accurate to the minute. I had no watch, but Juré kept a clock with a digital display beside his bed, and I checked the time whenever I made an entry in my notebook. That night, after Pirgi had enlisted me in his cause, Mr Schtetler was not home for dinner. It was at around eight that I noticed him come in, not because I saw him, but because the sound of the apartment door opening and closing was easy to hear. From the bedroom I heard him exchange some remarks with his wife. I was preparing an assignment for school, and I left the bedroom to get a drink of water and saw them together at the dining-room table. They stopped talking as I went into the kitchen, took a glass, and filled it with water. Mrs Schtetler smiled at me, but Mr Schtetler stared at the table and did not smile. When I got back to my room I heard the voices start up again. Their conversation was brief, and in a few minutes I heard the door open and close again. I had observed that Mr Schtetler had not taken off his coat while he spoke with his wife, and I made a note of this detail, thinking that it might be important.

I knew how delicate my position was. I could not afford to raise suspicions. That night I washed quickly and went to bed, wondering while I lay reading my book how late it would be when Mr Schtetler returned home. Juré went to bed shortly after I did, but he turned his light out immediately. From one of the other rooms I could hear the murmur of the television. I continued to read until, hours later, I started awake with the book lying open on my chest. Juré slept on. Afraid my light would bother him, I turned it off. It was now past midnight, and though I was almost certain that Mr Schtetler was not home yet, I couldn't be sure. I had no choice but to stay awake until either I heard him come in or somehow determined that he was already home.

I stared at the ceiling, which from time to time was illuminated by lights from traffic moving outside. At one point I got up and stood by the window, which looked over the front grounds of the building. The bedroom was cool, but I trembled because I was afraid that I had failed, that on the first night of my assignment I had allowed Mr Schtetler to return home undetected. As I stood by the window I composed in my head an appeal for forgiveness that I would present to Pirgi with my eyes cast downward and my bottom lip quivering. I sat on the bed, but stood again after only a minute when I felt my head grow heavy and my eyes begin to shut of their own accord. It was after three when finally a car pulled up on the street and I saw a slim figure emerge from the passenger side. In a few moments I heard the door of the apartment open and could be absolutely certain that Mr Schtetler had returned from his late-night adventures. I breathed a sigh of relief and went to bed.

The following day I overslept and had trouble paying attention in school. The next night was much the same. Mr Schtetler was out when I got home. He came in around nine, left again almost immediately and didn't return until after three in the morning. I made careful notes, but wondered if my lack of sleep was making me less observant than I had hoped to be. The next night Mr Schtetler actually joined us for dinner and spoke to me for the first time, asking me if I liked my school. I said yes and told him that I was much happier here than in the orphanage. After supper the boys asked me to go with them to the video arcade, but I was so tired I had to say no. They left and I went to my room to try to do some homework, but I couldn't concentrate. Mr and Mrs Schtetler were talking, and I heard her say that the money the state was paying them for keeping me was good money and that they couldn't afford to send me away. When Mr Schtetler answered, his voice was so low I couldn't understand what he was saying. I wrote down that he wanted to send me away and that she wanted me to stay. After this Mr Schtetler left.

I tried to work, but I must have fallen asleep, because when I looked up Mrs Schtetler was standing in the doorway watching me.

'You work too hard,' she said. 'My boys wonder if you are some sort of little genius sent to inspire them in their schoolwork.'

The notebook was open on the desk. I knew that if I tried to cover it I would only draw her attention to it.

'I want to do well. I'm not a genius. I have to work hard. I have no choice.'

'You will make yourself sick, working all the time like that.'

'I'm just tired. I haven't been sleeping.'

'It must be hard for you, living in all these strange places with people you don't know. I want you to feel at home here. We can give you food and keep you warm, but we'll never be like a real family to you. I can understand that.'

I nodded.

'I want you to feel that you can ask me for anything. I'll get it for you.'

I looked at her. I wasn't sure what she was trying to say.

'You know, like Coca-Cola or a new Walkman.' She shrugged. 'An American rock-music T-shirt.'

'I would like a glass of water.'

When she left the room I closed the notebook. She came back a moment later with a glass of cold water.

'I know boys your age have certain things that they want. Just let me know. Please.'

I smiled at her and when she left I put the notebook under my pillow. I was already so tired I didn't know how I was going to stay awake to keep my watch. I tried reading but immediately felt that familiar heaviness pressing down on my eyelids. I walked around the room, stood at the window. But even standing up I was falling asleep. After the boys returned from the video arcade there were voices and the sounds of people getting ready for bed. Someone turned on the television, but the noise lasted for only a few minutes, and soon there was nothing I could do to keep myself awake. I crawled into bed and was instantly carried away into a profound and dreamless slumber. The next thing I knew Juré was shutting off the alarm. I had slept through the night and heard nothing.

All day I worried about how to fill in the gap in my notes. I had two choices: tell Pirgi that I had fallen asleep and missed Mr Schtetler's arrival home the previous night, or make something up. If I told him the truth he would probably take the assignment from me and never speak to me again. I would be able to sleep through the night, but I would also have to bear the shame of failure. I thought about what I should do and late that afternoon decided that it would do no harm to simply put down that Mr Schtetler had arrived home shortly after three in the morning.

I had the page in my pocket when I walked past building P on the way home. Pirgi was talking to a man wearing a long mushroom-coloured coat. When I signalled to him from the street he motioned for the man to wait and came over to the fence.

'You have something for me?'

I took the paper out and pushed it through the wire fence into his fingers. He put it in his pocket without looking at it.

'I want you to know that your work is very important. I will pass this along. I don't have time to talk today because, as you can see, I am busy. But we will talk again soon. When you bring the next message. I promise.'

With this he smiled and gave me a wink before hurrying back to the waiting man. As they resumed their discussion they turned away from me and I could not see their faces. Pirgi gestured with his hands as if emphasizing a point. The man nodded.

I tried to control my disappointment, but all I could think was that he had approached me with an offer of companionship, and now he was dismissing me as if I were a servant. I held back my tears on the walk back to the Schtetlers' apartment, my eyes on the pavement, and once inside I went straight to my room.

That night I stayed awake until dawn waiting for the sound of Mr Schtetler returning. I fell asleep as it began to grow light, but I managed to wake in time for breakfast. When I went out to the kitchen I saw that Mr Schtetler was still not home. Mrs Schtetler did not seem worried, however, and so I concluded that she knew where he was and both expected and approved of his absence.

I went to school, but was so tired that I had trouble following what the teacher was saying and could not focus on the words written on the blackboard. I fell asleep in mathematics class and was sent to the nurse's office, where I explained that it had been weeks since I had been able to sleep soundly at night. I dozed off while she spoke with someone over the phone. Finally she wrote something on a piece of paper and told me to give it to Mrs Schtetler. Then she sent me home.

After I gave her the paper from the nurse, Mrs Schtetler went out for a while. She came back with some pills in a bottle and told me they would help me sleep, but I should take them only at night. I struggled to stay awake through dinner, and afterward Mrs Schtetler gave me one of the pills and sent me straight to bed. I didn't hear a thing the entire night and only awoke when Juré's alarm went off. Mr Schtetler could have come and gone a hundred times. But lack of sleep had left me so groggy I didn't care about Pirgi and whether or not Mr Schtetler was an anarchist.

I used a free period at school to fill up a page with notes about Mr Schtetler. Since I hadn't seen him for several days I made it all up. I wrote that on Sunday he came home at five in the afternoon, stayed in the apartment reading until midnight, and then went out. For Monday I wrote that he talked on the phone for two whole hours and then left the apartment after a late night phone call. I wrote that on Tuesday morning he ate breakfast with us and told jokes and made everyone laugh. I invented shadowy visitors and mysterious packages. I wrote whatever came into my head. When I gave this paper to Pirgi he told me I was a good boy and that we would talk again soon.

I was feeling much better. The pills helped me to sleep and I didn't worry about what Mr Schtetler was doing or how much time he spent away from home. I began to enjoy the company of the Schtetler boys, especially Juré, who was close to me in age, and through him I made some friends in the neighbourhood. We went out most evenings and roamed the streets, talking and laughing. I saw Pirgi whenever I passed by Building P, but never let on to anyone that I had spoken with him. He was almost always with someone, two or three young men with shaved heads wearing dark jackets, or else the man in the mushroom-coloured coat. Every week I found an opportunity to pass a piece of paper through the fence and into his stubby fingers. Each time he put it into his pocket without looking at it and told me I was a good boy. But after the first of these not a single word of truth was written on any of them.

Then one afternoon Pirgi wasn't there when I walked by Building P. I was alone and so I went through the break in the fence and looked around the grounds of the building. I sat on the bench where Pirgi had brought me to chat. The play area was still deserted and all the toys were still broken, and I noticed that the trees were losing their leaves. I had been sitting there for a while when a young girl walked by carrying a baby, but she only glanced at me and didn't say anything. Across the street a few children were playing in the parking lot. But there was no sign of Pirgi.

That evening I went to the video arcade with Juré and some of our friends. It was a chilly night and once we were finished playing our games I was eager to return to the Schtetlers' apartment and have a glass of warm milk before going to bed. However, there seemed to be some excitement among the other boys in our group, and before I could grab Juré's arm to get him to come with me, we were joined by some older boys and being swept along by a tide of anticipation. I moved to the middle of the crowd where I was warmed by the crush of bodies. The cold air was still and aromatic with cigarette smoke. I had been separated from Juré, but as we entered a narrow cobbled street he appeared by my side and told me that the police were out and that there was something going on near the ruins of the cathedral. Everyone was drawn by the danger and wanted to see what had happened, and I could tell by the way Juré's eyes shone in the light of the street lamps that I would not be able to convince him to leave and go home.

The echo of voices grew louder as we approached the cathedral.

When we rounded the corner and entered the square, there was suddenly so much light it was like the sun had come up. Several cars had been overturned and lit on fire. There were hundreds of people out, and many of them were chanting slogans that didn't make any sense to me. There were also police in the square, but they were just standing around, watching. I held Juré by the arm as the others pushed forward, and when we saw our chance we crept to the edge of the square and stood on the sidewalk, where the crowd was not as thick. We watched for several minutes, and then I noticed that there were men walking through the crowd with video cameras, filming the scene. I pointed this out to Juré and said I thought we should leave.

A lot of people were arrested, but this didn't end the disturbances, and after about two weeks the police imposed a curfew. I was glad that Mr Schtetler was not among those arrested, but my stay was cut short when the fighting started in earnest. The Schtetlers left the city and I returned to the care of the state.

Years later, after the government fell and during the time when nobody was in charge, I lived in a refugee camp in the mountains near the border. We were queuing for food when I noticed a small man in a black rubber rain suit waiting in another line. It was Pirgi. He stood with his face directed downward and his hands folded in front of him. When he reached the front of the line he took a plate from the stack and then looked back down at the ground. He walked with a limp and seemed to pull his left leg behind him. He spoke to no one. Once we had received our meal he retreated to a corner of the tent and sat on the ground to eat even though there were plenty of empty places at the tables. I took a seat close by. His face was a patchwork of scars and his hand shook when he raised the spoon to his mouth. I had spoken to many people about my experiences and had known for a long time that he was a police informant. But I wasn't angry. I only wished to discuss our common memories. I approached him, but the moment he saw me he dropped his plate and pulled himself to his feet. He looked so scared he seemed to be in pain. I hadn't intended to trouble him, so I just watched as he maintained the distance between us by circling one of the long tables. He crept along, keeping his eyes on me as he approached the exit of the tent. I didn't bother to follow, but after a minute went over to the exit and pushed back the flap. The last I saw of Pirgi, he was dragging his leg through the mud and the rain, along an obscure mountain path that, as far as I knew, didn't lead anywhere.

I had found an inexpensive apartment – a single room, with a sink, toilet and open shower stall in one corner behind a screen. It was on the second floor of an old stucco house on a cobbled lane that was too narrow for any vehicle other than a motor scooter. The houses along the lane butted against one another, crammed in like dirty, jagged teeth. Front doors opened right on the street. Just past the house where I had rented the apartment the street rose steeply all the way to the top of the hill, where the cathedral sat like a presiding deity, gazing down upon the town. If you weren't fit or if you took it too quickly, the climb could tire you out and leave you gasping. But I made this journey several times a day on my way to and from work and found it made the muscles in my legs firm and strong.

The house had been renovated cheaply many years ago by the owner, Mr Tsalimitris, who lived downstairs with his wife, Maria. They had two sons who had grown up and moved away, and as soon as they were gone Mr Tsalimitris converted their bedrooms into apartments and began taking in boarders. Mr and Mrs Tsalimitris were old now. He had once worked as a barber but was so unpopular that when another barbershop opened in the town he lost all his customers. He was bad tempered and always seemed to think people were trying to cheat him. When I gave him the first week's rent, he squinted and counted the money, note by note, not once but three times. Then he looked at me and said, 'I'll take your money and give you a place to sleep. But you are not welcome here.' He had a full head of unkempt silver hair and always wore an undershirt, long trousers, and sandals. His shoulders were thick and his arms bulky, giving the impression of strength. But he never seemed to do any work. If there was something heavy to lift or a nail to pound, you could be sure that it would be Mrs Tsalimitris doing the lifting or the pounding.

My job was to help the local prelate sort and catalogue an archive of documents that had been discovered in the basement of the cathedral after a flood. The documents were in many languages, but the job advertisement said that fluency in all of these languages was not a requirement. I later learned that it had been almost a year since they'd started looking for someone to do the work, but had been unable to find anyone with the desired linguistic skills. In desperation, they downgraded their requirements more than once, and by the time I came across the advertisement and answered it the job could have gone to almost anyone.

The interview was conducted by the prelate's assistant, a nervous and haughty young man with a narrow face and a sparse beard. He looked lost and underfed in his overlarge cassock. His office occupied one corner of a cramped book-lined space in the rectory behind the cathedral, and through his window I could see the town spread out around the hill, the whitewashed houses like dozens of sugar cubes spilled haphazardly across a sun-frazzled landscape.

Each morning I climbed the hill and, invigorated by the exercise, began my work at a desk in a windowless storage room on the rectory's second floor, where the documents had been placed while the flood was in progress. Many were damaged, some beyond repair. The paper and binding were in some cases hundreds of years old and had suffered greatly from being kept in a damp place that lacked ventilation. In the worst instances the ink had turned to dust and came away on my fingers or simply fell off the page. Sometimes, if the paper was particularly brittle or ravaged by mildew, it disintegrated, crumbling beneath my fingers like ash. The history of the town was obscure, and no one seemed to know where these volumes and piles of paper came from or what information they might contain. In the first days of my employment, as I tried to determine the nature and extent of the labour that lay ahead of me, I found that the cache of documents that had been preserved was a chaotic miscellany of ledgers, diaries, notebooks, inventories, correspondence, sermons, and lists of landowners, all of them written by hand on paper of varying quality. It was as if many people had died at once and, for lack of a reasonable alternative, all of their private papers had been thrust for safekeeping into the vaults beneath the cathedral, where the collection had lain mouldering and forgotten for centuries, until the October rains of the previous year had penetrated the cathedral walls and caused the prelate such panic that he ordered the doors to the vaults opened so the water could be drained and the damage assessed.

Though I was told to consider myself an employee of the prelate, answerable directly to him, I was to take my guidance from the prelate's assistant. From the day I was hired to the day I left, I saw the prelate only from a distance, was never invited to his office, and did not exchange a word with him. Perhaps because of this the nature of my duties remained vague, for the prelate's assistant was a busy man whose interest in the project I had been hired to undertake was minimal, and who did not provide specific directions that would aid me in completing my tasks. Though I often saw him giving instructions to the local women hired to clean and cook and perform the routine chores necessary for the parish house to function, he seemed to regard my questions as trivial and was content to let me determine which piles of paper were important and which were not.

I would rise as the sun came up and arrive at my desk no later than seven o'clock. Then I would spend the morning transcribing documents onto long pads of paper. I assigned each document a number and, in a separate booklet, recorded the number along with a brief description of the document's contents. Then I put the document and my transcription into a manila envelope, recorded the number on the outside, and placed the envelope on its edge on a shelf in the storage room. The prelate's assistant, who had devised this system, seemed to expect that when I was finished my work he would have at his fingertips a descriptive list that would lead him directly to whichever document he wanted. However, I could have told him early in my tenure that flaws in the process were going to make access to the documents circuitous and difficult. But other than acknowledging that I could read these pages of script while he could not, he did not credit me with much in the way of intelligence and, if I happened to make a suggestion that challenged his way of doing things, simply told me to follow the instructions I had been given.

At about midday, when the sun was at its height, I would leave my desk and visit a café in the town for lunch, and then return to my room for siesta, which would last for several hours. I was not used to this custom, and in the early days of my employment I regarded sleeping in the middle of the day as an extravagant waste of time. But I quickly discovered the advantage of two or three restful early afternoon hours. The temperature at midday could climb into the nineties or higher, making work that required close concentration impossible. After a few days of resisting the idea of siesta and finding my head nodding as my office turned into an oven, I gave in and passed the hottest hours of the day in my apartment asleep. At around five, refreshed and alert, I would return to my desk in the storage room, which had begun to cool, for several more hours of work. After that I was free to spend my evening as I liked.

One day I returned to find that Mr Tsalimitris had rented the other room on the second floor of his house. For some weeks I had been their only lodger, and I had grown used to a quiet household and uninterrupted sleep. My rent covered access to the kitchen on the main floor, though only during certain times of the day. Considering the modest sum I paid each week, it was generous of them to let me store food in their refrigerator and use their pots and pans. To be sure, the room I occupied was not much. The walls were bare. It lacked air conditioning. Its only furnishings were a bed not much wider than a cot, a flimsy bedside table, a chair with uneven legs, and a lamp. The single window looking out on the narrow street provided little relief from the heat of the day. In order to create a cross-breeze I had been keeping my door wedged open whenever I slept. Now, with someone in the room across the hall, I would have to keep the door closed. My disappointment became tinged with annoyance when I discovered that I would be sharing quarters with a woman and her two small children.

It was early evening and still light. She stood in the street with Mr Tsalimitris and was counting money, note by note, into his outstretched palm. The children, a boy and a girl, danced around her, clapping their hands, chanting a song in a language I could not identify. The day had been very hot. Mrs Tsalimitris stood just inside the door watching the children, a broad smile on her face. Unlike his wife, Mr Tsalimitris ignored the children, concentrating instead on the money the woman was giving him. I hurried by them.

'Good evening,' Mrs Tsalimitris said as she stepped aside to let me in.

'Hello,' I greeted her.

I went up the stairs to my room, closing and locking the door behind me. I sat on the bed and removed my shoes, relishing the relief of air on my tired feet. Tonight it was too hot to cook. In a short while I would venture into the town for supper. In the meantime I waited.

It wasn't long before they came upstairs. The children continued to chant and, as if it were a game, trod heavily upon each step until their mother scolded them. The door across the hall slammed behind them when they went inside. This was followed by loud conversation and childish laughter and other unidentifiable noises. I assumed their room was similar to mine, and the idea of it being occupied by three people was hard to imagine, even if two of them were children.

I was so agitated I was not thinking clearly when I went out for my evening meal. I chose a restaurant specializing in roast chicken that Mr Tsalimitris had suggested I try. It was, so he claimed, one of his favourite places to eat.

The tables were situated beneath a canopy of grape vines supported by wooden lattice, and were open to the air. People strolling by could look at the food being served, and if they liked what they saw they could enter and take a seat. Stray dogs and cats begging at the tables caused no concern among the restaurant staff. I had lit a cigarette and the waiter had just brought my beer when I saw her approaching, hand in hand with the children. I don't really mind children, but I don't know how to talk to them. It exhausts me to invent topics of conversation that will hold their interest, and I find their games and prattle tedious. I sipped my beer and watched her as she surveyed the menu. Silently I urged her to move on to the next restaurant. After heaving a sigh and counting the bills in her pocketbook, she herded the children ahead of her in among the tables nearest the street. A waiter came and escorted her toward the corner where I was seated. Next to me was a vacant table set for four. As she thanked him and they settled in, I raised my newspaper. The children whispered and giggled and kicked each other under the table.

'Look at the menu, please. Mischa, remember you don't like fish. So don't ask for fish like last time.'

Her voice was ragged with weariness and irritation. She sighed, and when she spoke next – sharply exhorting the children to behave themselves – it was in her own language, which, though I don't understand it, I recognized as Romanian. From this distance it was easy to observe her. She had plain broad Slavic features – a high fore-head, small eyes and upturned nose – and the pale skin of someone who does not spend much time out of doors. Her long black hair was tied behind her neck into a ponytail – not stylishly, but to keep it from her face. Her clothes were plain as well. Over her thickset body she wore a simple short-sleeved dress printed with small flowers and on her bare feet were a pair of those plastic sandals they sell at all the tourist kiosks. The children were more attractive. Mischa was seated with his back to me. He sat upright and held the menu as if it were a book. He had thin arms and shoulders and closely cropped blond hair. He would have been no more than six or seven. The girl was older, but not by more than a year or two. Her skin was also very pale and her hair dark, but where her mother appeared tired and bleached of colour, she was delicate and winsome. I turned back to my newspa-per, keeping one eye on her as she leaned across the table and, smiling, whispered something to her brother. Suddenly her eye caught mine. I looked away, but I could now sense her watching me, and Mischa turning in his chair to glance in my direction. I twisted my chair away from them and held the newspaper close to my face as if trying to con-centrate.

In a few moments the waiter brought my meal of roast chicken and fried potatoes, and after placing it in front of me turned to the next table to receive their orders. This did not take more than a few seconds as they all ordered roast chicken with fried potatoes. Once the waiter had gone I felt their attention shift more earnestly in my direction. The newspaper was folded next to my plate, and I bent my head over it. I hoped they would see that I was preoccupied and interested in what I was reading. But with each minute that passed, their whispers grew louder. I tried to ignore them and eat my meal, and eventually the waiter returned with three plates of roast chicken and fried potatoes. This occupied them for some minutes, and I convinced myself they had forgotten me. But when I had picked clean the last bones on my plate and laid down my knife and fork, the mother spoke.

'Excuse me?'

I didn't hurry to respond. I kept my eyes on the newspaper, and only after several seconds did I turn to face her.

'Yes?'

'I am sorry,' she said. 'I am sorry if I bother you. My children are telling me you stay in same house with us. The one of Mr Tsalimitris and his wife. I did not see you there so I say they are wrong. But they say it is the truth. So I am sorry if it is not true and I bother you for nothing.'

'That's where I'm staying,' I said, since it was pointless to deny it. 'Your children are right. I thought I saw you earlier today, but I wasn't sure.'

I glanced at the children as she smiled and nodded. Both were watching me with stony faces.

'My name is Sonya,' she said, extending her hand, which I took into mine and squeezed lightly. 'Sonya Georgescu. This is my son Mischa, my daughter Peta.'

'Kostandin Bitri,' I said. Both children held their hands toward me and I had to reach across the table to grasp them.

'Do you work here in this town?' asked Sonya, as she picked up her knife and fork and resumed her meal. 'Or are you visit?'

'I have a job with the prelate's office,' I told her.

She nodded. 'It is not easy thing, to find job,' she said. 'I look hard. I fill out many forms. But with language, it is a problem. Always, they want me to speak with better words, and always they want English. Because of guests, you know?'

'Do you work in a hotel?'

She seemed confused and hesitated before answering.

'We are here to visit,' she said. 'Holiday. We are take time and look at things and eat in restaurant.'

'But back home,' I clarified. 'Do you work in a hotel? You said there were guests.'

Again, my question seemed to cause her difficulty and I wished I had not asked it.

'My husband,' she said finally.

'Oh, so he works in a hotel.'

She looked at me and glanced quickly from side to side, as if she'd said more than she'd intended or thought someone was listening. In the space of only a few minutes Mischa and Peta had eaten every scrap of food on their plates, but both now sat looking down at the table and not saying a word.

'It doesn't matter,' I said. 'I'll let you get back to your food.' The waiter was approaching again and I took out my wallet to pay the bill.

'Mr and Mrs Tsalimitris are very nice people,' Sonya remarked, smiling once more, her uncertainty of a moment ago melting away.

'Yes,' I said, going along with her even though I thought Mr Tsalimitris was bigoted, greedy and lazy, and his wife was stupid.

'Our room, it is very nice. Clean and nice, with hot water.'

I gave the waiter some money and waved him away when he offered to make change.

'Yes, so is mine,' I said. When I stood, both Peta and Mischa looked up at me and I saw in the glance of each an emotion that fell somewhere between hope and fear, something that made me think the whole family had been travelling for a long time and that, out of necessity or by default – certainly not by choice – this tiny backward town represented for them a final refuge.

'You go home now, back to room?' Sonya asked.

'Maybe,' I said. 'Enjoy your dinner.'

'Bye, bye,' Peta said.

Mischa said, 'Bye, bye.'

I waved to them and tried to appear casual as I left the restaurant.

But in my desperation to escape I must have hurried my pace, for as I turned down the street I nearly collided with an old woman dressed entirely in black. She cried out as I twisted to avoid her, and I could still hear her muttering as, without apology, I walked away.

At the end of the street I ducked into a narrow pathway dividing two rows of buildings. It was absurd, but I felt a strong compulsion to keep moving, almost as if I were being followed. Not until I'd turned three more corners and was lost within this labyrinth of winding passageways did I slow down.

Nobody was behind me. I had stumbled into a residential quarter of the town. Here and there an elderly man or woman sat on the front step of a house and observed me as I went by. Almost all the windows and doors I passed were open, and the air was fragrant with the aroma of meals being prepared. I didn't speak or even meet anyone's eyes. I kept moving, more from embarrassment than for any other reason, because everyone could see I was lost. But after wandering aimlessly for a few minutes I noticed a familiar landmark, then another. And when I emerged from between two buildings into an open square, it revealed itself as the one closest to the foot of the hill I climbed each day to go to work.

I went to a café that had a roof garden, ordered a drink of rakí and water, and took it upstairs. The garden provided a view of the square and from my table I could see people coming and going, moving in all directions. It was the beginning of the tourist season and each day buses brought them in from the larger towns to buy the local crafts, gaze at the historical artefacts in the tiny museum, and wander through the cathedral. Most of the people milling about the square had spent all day here and were waiting for their buses to return. Hundreds of years ago during the time of the Venetian occupation the town had been the stronghold of a feudal lord and had been fortified and enclosed by a high stone wall with battlements. Frequent attack and invasion had left the outer wall in fragments, and in later years many of the stones were hauled away and used to build houses. Today, though there was nothing left but remnants covered with grass and weeds, the tourist literature boasted of the historical significance of the town and its wall. Visitors flocked in only to find themselves staring at piles of rocks and broken mortar: all that remained of the great structure that had once protected the local population from enemy forces.

I finished my drink and ordered another. The sky was beginning to dim, and I wondered how Sonya had found her way to such an obscure and inconsequential place. If it was work she was after, she would do much better in the city or one of the nearby towns where there were more opportunities and where her status as a foreign national would not be held against her to the degree that it would be here. If she had no permanent visa she would have to accept a lower wage than a local, but surely she knew that already. Because of her confusion earlier this evening I was not convinced that her situation was as simple as it appeared she wanted me to believe. What was a Romanian woman, who didn't know if she was looking for work or not, doing with her children in a place like this? I did not know how long she planned to stay, but unless she had struck a special deal with Mr Tsalimitris, the terms of her occupancy were the same as mine: rental by the week with the requirement of a full seven days' notice before leaving. This was not an arrangement a tourist would make. But since I had no intention of getting involved, I put her out of my mind. I lit a cigarette, sipped my drink and enjoyed the scenery.

The sky dimmed further and soon it was dark. The buses had come and retrieved the tourists and the square was empty but for a few old men sitting in their chairs in front of a taverna. I was on my fifth glass of rakí when Sonya, holding Peta and Mischa by the hand, entered the square. They went straight across the cobbles and up the lane that led to the Tsalimitris residence. After they were gone I waited fifteen minutes before paying for my drinks and leaving the café. As I staggered back to my room I wondered if this was the schedule I would have to keep in order to avoid spending all my evenings in the company of Sonya, Mischa and Peta Georgescu.

A few days later I found the first of the diary pages. I was transcribing a volume filled with page after page that in three columns listed household items purchased, the vender who sold the goods, and the corresponding expense. It was late in the morning and as the temperature rose toward its midday zenith my mind began to wander. The heat was making it more and more difficult to concentrate on what I was supposed to be doing. But, to be fair to myself, I had not been sleeping well. Since the arrival of Sonya and her children, I had been keeping my door closed and locked at night, with the result that my room lost very little of the heat it gathered during the day. It was not that I wanted no contact with her, but she seemed lonely and I sensed something very like desperation in her glance whenever her eyes met mine. Instinct told me that she would unburden herself at the least provocation, and thereafter I would be enlisted in her cause and have no time for my own affairs. Each evening I ate at a different restaurant, and then stayed out until late, drinking. By the time I returned to my room, Sonya, Peta and Mischa were safely bedded down. I usually dropped off to sleep immediately, but at some point during the night would awaken in a sweat, hardly able to draw the warm stale air into my lungs. I found no solace in the idea of lighting a cigarette and sitting by the window. I did not want to disturb my hosts, which I would surely do if I began pacing the length of the room on creaky floorboards. I did not want to read, since I spent my days reading and was suffering eyestrain as a result. And so after dousing my head with cold water from the tap and performing a few brisk callisthenic exercises, I would crawl back into bed and stare at the ceiling until the eastern horizon began to brighten and I could shower and dress and venture down to the kitchen to fry a couple of eggs for my breakfast.

It was on a day that began in this fashion that I found the first of many leaves of brittle paper bearing eccentric, childish handwriting. It was tucked into the pages of the ledger I was transcribing, and at first I thought it was simply a sheet someone had inserted to mark the place. I was about to discard it when the words written at the top of the page caught my eye: *... in this world. I will defy them to my last breath. They cannot force me to love when there is not and never will be any love. I will see God first rather that give in to their demands.* The language was a variant of the local dialect, one that had not been in widespread use for at least a hundred years. But it was the writing itself that was most remarkable. First, it slanted to the left rather than to the right, and in places slanted so far as to lie almost flat on the line. And second, something about the style – the high lazy loops, the accents drawn with precise care instead of being blotted approximately into place – seemed to indicate an immature hand. Upon reading these lines I felt – the old cliché being true after all – my heart skip a beat in recognition of something, I wasn't quite sure what. I allowed myself an upward glance, to take in the room, the shelves of envelopes containing the hundreds of soulless, tiresome documents I had spent almost four months transcribing, before setting aside the ledger and returning to this page. I began a new sheet of paper and made my transcription with difficulty.

Today Father cursed me for being, as he put it, a child of Satan. Even Mother gasped in horror at this. Then, after he had gone, she said he had spoken rashly, not out of hatred but out of love. I asked her what kind of love condemns its child to a life without love? What kind of father entrusts his only daughter to the care of a murderer? She was crying, and when I thought of all the tears I have shed I was not sorry to see her bearing her portion of misery. Then I thought, and maybe I am evil for thinking so, that she cries knowing it kills me to see her thus and hopes to persuade me in this way to do Father's bidding. And then I thought, there is no pain. She pretends. But that was hours ago. It is night and the walls are silent and I pray that soon I will be delivered from my torment. I must …

The reverse was blank. The paper had a musty smell but had been protected from further damage by the ledger, where it had left a shadow on the pages between which it was concealed. The left-hand edge was irregular, the other smooth, indicating it had been torn from a volume. I turned back to the ledger and leafed through it carefully. Near the back I found a second sheet, the same dimensions as the first and bearing writing in the same hand.

… family as high as I should. That I am selfish and ungrateful. But I tell

him it is he who is ungrateful because he is willing to barter his daughter for useless wealth. There will always be another chance to build wealth, but where will he get another daughter once he has lost the first? To this he has no answer, except that I must be mad to believe the tales of goatherds and allow into my head these foolish notions of romance. 'Happiness,' he tells me, 'is doing God's will. Freedom is duty. Your life is not your own. Remember that.' He leaves me. Below my window, people carry on with the business of putting enough food on the table to keep themselves alive. To them, my plight would seem absurd. They would laugh to hear of a girl who refuses to even meet the man her father has chosen for her husband. 'You have enough to eat,' they would say. 'What is your problem?' And perhaps they ...

Unwillingly I left the storage room, already late for lunch and siesta.

That evening I returned to the storage room with the purpose of locating more pages from this document – the diary of a young girl or woman. I tried to remember where I had found the ledger, thinking that volumes stored next to it might also contain loose pages. This, of course, was a fallacy because the documents had been stacked haphazardly at the time of the flood, and then rearranged a number of times to allow for the drying process. By any standard of manuscript preservation or rescue it was not an ideal state of affairs. I had noticed dampness in the pages of some volumes when I had done my original inventory and had placed these where they would be exposed to the air. But because there were too many damp volumes and not enough room to spread them out, I could see that trying to save these volumes was futile. The prelate's assistant had been quite clear that he did not want the documents straying from this room, leaving me with the sole option of laying volumes open on their spines for a day or two in any available space I could find, then putting these away while opening others in their place. I left a narrow path of clear floor between the door and my desk, but otherwise the room was filled with documents, either stacked against the wall or open on the floor. I realized that moving volumes around like this and laying them flat was probably causing damage to the bindings, but didn't see any other way to get the job done.

But now the focus of my assignment had changed. Until I happened upon the pages of the diary I had not been fully engaged by anything I had read: list after list of household items, deeds describing the location and boundaries of property, notarized agreements documenting the sale of land and animals. The occasional parish record listing births and deaths, or a complaint that someone had registered against someone else, came as a godsend simply on the basis of human interest. But much of what I found was dry as bone, and the task of transcribing it pure drudgery. So the girl's voice echoed in my mind long after I had read her words. Not only that, but her misfortune made me indignant. I thought of her all the time. Visions of her occupied my dreams.

I did not find any more pages of the diary that night or for several days following the initial discovery. I had finished with the ledger and was working on a bundle of loose pages that appeared to be the remnants of a family genealogy when I noticed a fragment of textured paper lying on my desk. The paper from the diary was distinctive: creamy with flecks of colour floating in it. And when I compared this bit of paper with the two pages I had already found, I knew that I was close to discovering another. There were none hidden within the pages of the genealogy, but when I returned to the stack that the genealogy had come from, I was rewarded with a vision that almost made me weep, for beside it on the floor lay another small three-cornered scrap of cream-coloured paper. With great care I lifted the entire stack of random documents into my arms and brought them to my desk, where I spent the remainder of the morning and all that evening sorting through them. When I was done I had no fewer than twenty-five diary pages. Some were complete and others fragmentary. But I had enough, I hoped, to enable me to piece together the girl's story from beginning to end.

Though I was still not sleeping well, I began to relax and not worry so much about everything, including the inevitable intrusions of Sonya and her children into my daily life. I worked on my transcription of the diary pages and did not put myself to any trouble to avoid her. Sometimes I ate breakfast with her, and one afternoon spent a friendly hour with her and Mischa and Peta at a café that specialized in cream-filled sweets. She told me about her life in Bucharest and said that her husband had suggested she take the children on vacation since he was going to be busy all summer with his government work. I tried to speak with the children, but because their English was poor they were mostly silent and simply nodded and smiled. I was able to teach them a few words – cat, dog, dress, table. But for conversations to take place we had to rely upon their mother to translate. I did not worry that Sonya's story was filled with contradictions and inconsistencies, that one day she could say she taught arithmetic to fourth-graders and on another that she worked as a typist in an office; that her parents had died in a train wreck years ago and that they were living happily in an apartment in Timisoara; that life in Romania was improving and that people had to stand in line for hours just to buy a roll of toilet paper. I did not worry that she and her children seemed to spend much of their time confined to their room and that what they were doing with all these daylight hours was as mysterious as their origins. Much of what she told me she simply volunteered. I didn't ask her many questions, because I noticed early on that her idea of a dialogue was in fact a monologue. I could attend to these conversations with only half an ear because she did not seem to be looking to me for input. Indeed, if I had bothered to think about it, I might have guessed she was in rehearsal for something, trying out a variety of stories to see how they would play. But I was hardly listening, and at times my distraction was complete as I mused upon what I had learned from the diary.

Working on the diary required sustained concentration and stamina. The writing in places was illegible; some pages were heavily stained or foxed, some were fragmentary. There were days when I worked through two pages in the morning, but on others it took me all day just to decipher a few lines. It was also not helpful that the pages as I had found them were not in any particular order and that, not having any idea how long the complete document might have been I could not tell how much was missing. However, by the time I had transcribed the last word on the last page, I was confident I had learned the essential details of the story.

The girl was Anna-Sophia Ghirlandaio, the only daughter of Alessandro Ghirlandaio, a nobleman whose estate incorporated towns and villages for many miles in every direction. He was a man accustomed to having his way in all things, a faithful and generous friend, a ruthless enemy. His land holdings were his life and he provided protection to those who lived on and worked his land. He had his own standing army, a force so powerful even the Pope feared and respected him. When he was young he married the daughter of a man whose smaller estate he coveted, and by this union he became the most powerful landowner in the empire. His wife, however, was not strong and nearly died giving birth to their first child, a daughter. Anna-Sophia was the only child she would bear. Alessandro gave the girl everything, the best education, all the amusements and luxuries she could desire. He was grooming her, not to take over from him, but to marry well and provide him with a son-in-law whom he could designate his heir. When Anna-Sophia was sixteen he found a suitor for his daughter, Tomasso Gozzoli, a wealthy shipbuilder and slave trader who was in a position to extend Alessandro's empire across the sea and bring riches from other lands. Though Gozzoli was charming and ambitious and willing to go along with Alessandro's plan, there was a problem. He was already married, to a woman who had regretted the union almost immediately after it had taken place and entered a convent to escape her husband. Alessandro was ignorant of this previous marriage, but since Gozzoli had already petitioned the Vatican to have the marriage annulled and been refused, the word was sure to get out. Not about to let a youthful indiscretion thwart his ambitions, Gozzoli made arrangements to have the problem taken care of, and the story spread about was that the woman had grown despondent and thrown herself from the chapel's bell-tower. When Alessandro told his daughter of the upcoming betrothal he was prepared for some resistance because Anna-Sophia was wilful, impetuous and independent-minded, but it was only after taking a walk in the fields that she announced to her father that she would have nothing to do with Tomasso Gozzoli, a known murderer. Where did she get such a story, her father demanded to know. And then it came out, about the goatherd who was also a monk. She had paid many visits to his hovel, where they spent hours discussing God and love and the nature of good and evil. He had told her, she said, about Gozzoli's part in the death of his wife, but had advised her to accept the marriage anyway, because to refuse it would be a foolish act of selfishness that would bring about her own death. However, Anna-Sophia declared she could not marry the man and refused to even meet him. She would marry for love or not at all. This was the beginning of the standoff between father and daughter. Alessandro had the monk brought before him, questioned him, and sent him home to the charred remnants of his hovel and the slaughtered carcasses of his goats. Anna-Sophia was confined to a room in the fortress, provided with food and water, and permitted an hour in the courtyard each day and visits from her mother. She would remain there, her father told her, until she changed her mind.

... in the event that this room becomes my burial chamber. But the futility of writing stares me in the face each time I take the book out of its hiding place. Father will get his way. I imagine him disposing of me and hiring another girl to take my place, one who has no such qualms about marrying a wealthy murderer. I am afraid of him, my own father. I wonder if Gozzoli ever considers the pain he has caused. His dead wife. How many others have crossed him and bear the scars of his anger? Now I ask, do I acquiesce to save myself? Or do I defy the forces that are assembled against me? I do not know what I should do. Every day I pray for guidance but God is silent, offers no comfort, no advice. I am denied peace and think only death will bring the kind of peace I crave, but I do not want to die. There is much that I could do were I free. I believe if I dissemble, make peace with Father, promise to marry Gozzoli, and then flee before the nuptials ...

But even with all I had discovered, the puzzle was not yet complete. I hungered to know more. Above all else, I wanted to share my findings with someone. What I needed was confirmation that I had found something significant that would be recognized as such beyond the room where I worked, possibly beyond the town walls. Since I had no other contacts in the community, I made an appointment to see the prelate's assistant at his earliest convenience.

That evening I ate a meal of lamb stew with orzo, accompanied by a bottle of the local red wine. The air was unusually chilly for the time of year and I had to wear a fleece-lined jacket. I did not encounter Sonya or anyone else I knew as I left the restaurant and wandered down one lane and up another. I was thinking about Anna-Sophia. By now, I had formed a solid visual impression of her. She was of slight build with fair skin. Her long hair was the rich shade of chestnuts and her eyes the intense dazzling blue of the summer sky. When she cried she did so in silence, the tears flowing unchecked down her face and falling from her chin. But she did not cry often, only when she thought of how she was wounding others by holding so strongly to her convictions. An image that came to me often was of her reading a slim volume of poetry by candlelight and wearing a gown of silk brocade embellished with raised patterns woven in golden thread. During her walks in the courtyard she wore burgundy velvet slippers. She strolled along a cobbled footpath, pausing from time to time to admire the plentiful blossoms of the hyacinth and rosebushes, to gaze at the bougainvillea that clung to the stone walls and trailed upward to the gallery railing, and to observe the fish in a small pond. She was alone, but over her shoulder, hovering near a doorway, one could just make out the shadowy figure of a guard. In some of my dreams she appeared before me writing in a small leather-bound volume, using a quill tipped with ink; in others she sat before the window, her arms folded on the sill, her chin resting on her arms. I don't know where any of this came from, because the diary did not mention details of this nature, but these final two visions especially rendered themselves with such vivid clarity that I could scarcely believe I was imagining them and not somehow tapping into the celestial airwaves, as it were, and glimpsing events as they were unfolding.

I was awakened in the night by a sound at my door. The room had cooled, allowing me to sleep, and I was not happy to be disturbed. At first I thought it was the scratching of a mouse or rat beneath the floorboards, but as I floated toward consciousness it became apparent that someone was tapping on the door. It was still dark and when I checked my watch I saw it was only minutes past midnight. I pulled on my tattered dressing gown and opened the door.

Sonya stood in the hall. She wore a white bathrobe and on her feet were plain backless slippers. The door to her room was closed.

'I am very sorry to bother you,' she said in a whisper. She stared at my chest and seemed unable to lift her eyes to meet mine. 'But I need help. Advice. I must to ask you questions about what I should do.'

I stood back and let her into my room. I said nothing as I offered her the chair. She sat down. I sat opposite her on the bed. Moonlight entered through the window and bathed the side of her face in a silver glow.

She sighed and looked up at me with a timid smile. 'Where to start.' She seemed to wipe tears from her eyes, though I didn't see any. 'I tell you stories that are not true. I do not like to do this. Mischa and Peta see their mother telling lies. All the time I tell lies. What they think of me I do not want to know.' She paused again. 'But this is not for you to hear. What I have to say is this. We are from Romania. That part is true. I have passport to prove. We have been in this country for almost six months and soon they will send us back. I do not want to go. It is dangerous for us. People think our country has changed, and some things have changed since the Communists go away. But not everything. It is not what you call open society, like here. There are people looking out and watching, not like before with the Securitate and everybody watching everybody else. But there is secret police everywhere still. It is not safe to say some things. Conversation is reported. In old days, if you have typewriter, the authorities, they take great interest and make record in book that you have this and they want to see what you are writing. Only they could hand you out things you need like paper and ink ribbons. In those days television was not allowed. These are different now, but government still controls what we do and where we go. All the time we pay bribes. It was with lies that we leave country, saying we go for three weeks to visit relation. My husband, he knew they were going to find him, and he told us to go and not come back. He would follow, he said. But he has now been arrested and I hear nothing. You see, my husband was working for Ceausescu in old days. He was diplomat. Not Securitate. Not police. He was in position to invite guests in his house from other countries. He work for foreign services as liaison. It was like hotel, as you ask when we talk. You say he work in hotel and I thought maybe you know about me. Then we talk later and I see you do not know, you are not watching me for them. I think you are not. But I tell you now, my husband's work was in foreign service inviting government people from other countries to Romania. He was to increase trade, exports, that sort of thing. I did not know this when we marry. I did not know he work for Ceausescu. But his name, it is written down in old papers and they are releasing papers now, for anyone to see. His name, they find it in papers and one day there are men at door. They ask me questions I do not know answers. Friendly men with smiles, but they are the worst because they know you do not trust them and they do not care. My husband was not at home when they come because he work with importing company and have office in building. I telephone him and say these men come to house. You see, I am crying because I do not understand. My husband is very silent and he hangs up telephone. This is how it happens. One day, life is good and then everything is wrong. We have house, we have car. The children are in school. I do not see my husband for two days after visit from men and I am worried. You see how I should be worried. It is not for two days and I am coming home from buying food at store with Mischa and Peta when I see we are followed. Man in dark coat. I see him outside our house smoking. He does not hide. I think he wants me to see, so I know. My husband, he comes to back door in middle of night. I cry for joy to see him because I am thinking then he is already under arrest. But he tells me they will not arrest him that day because they think he will lead them to others. He is watched too. They follow him from office. They see everything. He tells me I must leave country or I will be arrested. I must take children and go. Hurry, he says. There is no time. I did not realize but he has been keeping passports. Always without telling me he has passports ready for us to escape. Make up story, he says. Leave country and I follow when I can. This is what he says. Then he goes. I do not see him again. I follow what he tells me to do. I get travel papers and tell them my cousin where she lives in Bulgaria invites us to stay. They want name and all information, and this I make up because I have no cousin. Three weeks is all I get. We cross border into Bulgaria, and that is not problem, but then I have to leave Bulgaria too because I see men follow us everywhere. I don't know what else I should do. It is luck that we can get out of Bulgaria because we go at night and in the rain, they just send us through. Stamp papers and no one looks or cares. For months we are going from town to town. I still think I see men following, but I am not sure. Sometimes there are men. Then there are no men. But now I have new problem. I apply for permission to stay for longer time but I hear nothing, and I think this is because we move around and never stay in one place. So I take room here and send message to immigration bureau that I want to increase time for visit and get special visa so I can work, because, you see, I have almost no money now after many months. But, and this is what they say, I need sponsor to say that I am good for to live and work in this country. Someone to say I am good person and not thief or watching for Romanian government.'

During much of this narration she gazed steadily at her clenched hands in her lap. But now she lifted her eyes and looked into mine.

'I know is much to ask. This I understand. But is important to me and my children that we stay and I find job. You have job with church doing papers. If you tell them you know of me and that I need from them to sign government form. It is all I ask. It cost them nothing. And then I can stay. My children will be safe?'

I nodded. I was hardly in a position of influence, but I could see no reason to turn down her request.

'I'll see what I can do,' I said. And when she reached across the space that separated us and gripped my hands, I added, 'But you know that I can't guarantee anything?'

'You are good man, Kostandin Bitri,' she said, her voice rising above the level of a whisper. She continued gripping my hands and rocking a bit in the chair as she gazed at me in the dusky light. I returned her gaze, relieved that she was asking no more than this and that with little inconvenience to myself I would be able to accommodate her. After a moment she gave my hands a final squeeze and leaned back.

I saw her to the door. She said nothing further, but the alarm was gone from her manner. She seemed serene, comforted by my promise to intercede on her behalf. We said goodnight to each other and as I was about to close the door she grasped my arm, raised herself on her toes, and kissed my cheek. I watched as she turned from me and entered her room. Then I closed the door and went back to bed.

I sat in the antechamber waiting for the prelate's assistant to see me. It was a clear, sunny day. The temperature had rebounded to above seasonal levels. By seven that morning the heat in the storage room was already suffocating. My mission was now twofold: to present the material I had found regarding Anna-Sophia Ghirlandaio and to plead the case of Sonya Georgescu. I had seen Sonya at breakfast and she had given me the paper requiring the signature, a document supporting her application for a work visa. Over eggs and bacon she smiled at me in a different way than before, and I have to admit I was not upset by this. I felt close to her, almost as if we shared a secret. She had taken me into her confidence and I had sworn to myself if not to her that I would do everything in my power to help her. It was not that I felt responsible, but I was convinced she did not deserve the fate that awaited her should she be designated undesirable and sent back to Romania.

I waited almost an hour before being shown into the office. The prelate's assistant was not at his desk, but after a few moments he bustled in from a side entrance. His cassock swept dramatically across the floor.

'I'm sorry to keep you waiting like this,' he said as he took his seat. He stroked his beard and regarded me with a grave expression. 'This is a busy week. But I'm glad you've come because there's something I must tell you.'

'Yes?'

He drew a piece of paper from a manila envelope and consulted it. 'You've been with us for almost five months.' He glanced at me. 'How far along are you with the project?'

I shrugged. 'A quarter or a third. No more than that. It's difficult work.' I looked at him. 'Laborious. Time-consuming.'

He held up his hand. 'Oh, you don't have to justify yourself to me, Mr Bitri. We set you a task that not many people would even attempt. And we're grateful for your efforts. It's just that, well, His Holiness expected the work to be done by now and I'm finding it hard to justify the expense. We're a small parish and our budget has already taken a beating from the damages done by the flood. I'm afraid that I'm going to have to ask you to finish up what you're doing sooner than expected. By the end of the week in fact. The project will have to be put into abeyance until there are funds available to spend on it. I'm sorry. This comes as a shock, I know. But it's out of my hands. It's the numbers talking. And they say we can't afford you right now.'

'Um,' I said. I nodded.

'We'll give you a good reference and maybe that will help you find another translating job.'

I had understood from the beginning I would not be working here forever. After all, the project was finite. There were only so many documents. But this was not expected. I looked at him. Already my mind raced with thoughts of all the things I would have to do.

'Now, you came to see me because you had something to discuss.'

'Yes,' I said. I shook my head, trying to bring myself back to what had seemed important a few minutes ago. I handed him the folder containing my transcription of the diary pages. He opened it and leafed through some of the sheets.

'What is this?'

'Have you ever heard of Anna-Sophia Ghirlandaio?' I asked.

He looked at me. 'It's a local legend. The girl was mistreated by her parents and took revenge by murdering them with poison. Then she disappeared.' He smiled. 'Not a story that inspires much of a moral example I'm afraid.'

I stared at him. He dropped the papers on the desk.

'If you go to the museum you'll find a lock of hair that's supposed to be hers. Not that there's any evidence she or anyone else actually did these things. Scholars think it was all made up to frighten the ignorant masses or incite rebellion. Her father was a bit of an autocrat by all accounts. He wanted her to marry some fellow and she refused, so he had her locked up. This went on for five years or ten years, depending on who's telling the story. In the version I heard she seduced one of her guards and escaped, but not before using hemlock she had gathered in the courtyard of the fortress to poison her father's wine supply. There were poems written about her. The story inspired all kinds of romantic rubbish over the years. It still circulates in one form or another but as you can imagine it's not easy to extract the truth out of all that fiction.'

I pointed toward the folder resting on his desk. I said weakly, 'I think I found her diary.'

He grimaced and shook his head.

'I wouldn't put much store in that. The story was there for anyone to make use of. If you found some sort of narrative account it was most likely written by someone using the legend as the basis for a novel. There are plenty of those in existence. I'm surprised you're finding that sort of thing. I'd have thought those papers would yield something a bit more useful than fodder for adolescent fantasies.'

He pushed the folder back to me across the desk.

'Was there something else?'

'Yes,' I said, trying not to sound shaken. I handed him the support document that Sonya had given me that morning. His habitual frown deepened to a scowl as he looked it over. 'Someone I know wants to apply for a work visa and she needs a sponsor to vouch for her good character. I was hoping you could ask the prelate to sign the form and send it in. It would save her from having to return to Romania and face possible arrest.'

He looked up at me. 'Arrest? What has she done?'

'Nothing,' I assured him. I gripped the edge of the desk and gave him a summary of Sonya's predicament, emphasizing the dangers from which she had already escaped and mentioning her children more than once. While I spoke he laid the form on his desk and folded his hands on top of it. I was not encouraged to see a smile spread slowly across his lips.

'I can see you know this woman well. Exactly how close are you?'

'We're friends.'

He nodded. 'And what skills does she bring with her? What can she do to earn her keep?'

I shrugged. 'I'm sure she'd be willing to do just about anything –'

He raised his hand.

'I'll stop you there. First of all, we're not running a diplomatic service. It's an affront to the office of His Holiness to expect him to take on an immigration case. Second, there are official channels that people follow when they want to come to this country and work. Hundreds – no, I would estimate thousands of people follow those channels every year. They fill out the proper forms and they get their permission legally. It's not my place to help someone circumvent the system.' At this point I tried to speak, but he held his hand up higher and raised his voice. 'No. Listen. Thirdly, you think you know this woman, but you really don't. Maybe she seduced you and now you find yourself obliged to argue her case. Or maybe you just feel sorry for her. I'll tell you something. You're not the first. She's tried this before. I guarantee it. And after the failure of this attempt she'll try again. These people are fundamentally dishonest. If she's deported, so much the better. You can't let yourself be taken in by an attractive woman telling a sad story. Give yourself more credit than that.'

When I looked at him again he was holding the paper toward me. I took it.

'I'd ask that when you fill out the termination forms you leave them with my secretary. Your last day is Friday. I'll have your reference letter ready by then. Is there anything else?'

I stood. 'I don't think so.'

'Then you should try to get some work done before lunch. I find these summer days pass by much too quickly. But when it's hot like this it's difficult to function. I'm not looking forward to my appointments this afternoon.'

'Would it help if she came and spoke to you herself?'

He'd stood as well and had been busy reading notes and shuffling papers from one corner of his desk to another, but with my question he became still and glanced my way.

'It's not my function, I'm afraid, to deal with people like that. If I spoke hastily I'm sorry. I'm sure her case is a strong one.'

He stared at me until I nodded and left.

I returned to my desk. In less than a minute the heat had enveloped me, fogging my mind and dulling my senses. Inevitably, my mind returned to the interview. I tried to remember what I'd said and where I had made my mistake. How, I wondered, could I have let myself in for such a thrashing?

I let my gaze wander around the stuffy room, the heat pressing down on me like a solid weight on my shoulders. Before me on the desk were the genealogy I had lately resumed work on, the folder containing my transcription of the pages from the diary, and the paper Sonya had given me. A part of me felt swayed by each of these to take up my pen and either perform some of the work I had been hired to do, or else make my petitions, on my own and Sonya's behalf, this time in written form directly to the prelate. But the truth was I had no heart for any of these things. What I wanted was a drink.

I left the rectory and walked down the hill into town. At the café I ordered a rakí, and when I had finished it I ordered another. The heat was insufferable. In a short time my shirt was soaked with perspiration. I knew that the alcohol was making it worse, but I didn't care. All I wanted was to escape my failures. After a third rakí I ordered a beer to soothe my throat. When I finished the beer I scattered some coins on the table and left the café.

I wandered the narrow shaded pathways of the town. I had no destination in mind, but somehow – either by subconscious design or by fluke – I found myself nearing the street where the museum was located. I followed the signs and was soon standing outside the little whitewashed building that housed the town's historical relics.

When I entered, a woman at a desk nodded to me and pressed a button on a hand-held counter. The room was pleasantly cool. I wandered through the brightly lit space, which I shared with about a dozen tourists, staring at a hotchpotch of objects sealed within Perspex cases: clay artefacts from Greek and Roman times, rusted weapons of more recent vintage, ecclesiastical robes and vestments, a communion vessel reputedly blessed by Pope Gregory VII in 1075, a Nazi helmet with a bullet hole through the right temple, a document dated 1838 marking the end of hostilities with the Ottoman Empire. In the far corner of a second room I found the object to which the prelate's assistant had made reference: a lock of hair preserved in a clear glass box. The hair was dark but faded and above it, inside the case where it was housed along with a number of other unrelated objects, was posted the following typewritten note: 'Hair said to be from the head of Anna-Sophia Ghirlandaio (c 1511–?), known as the "Witch of Tivoli" because of her use of poisons. Murdered her father, the nobleman Alessandro Ghirlandaio (c 1484–1534) and her mother. See Andros, César, *The Witch of Tivoli* (1877).' I reread these words until their meaning was lost in a blur of symbols, and then I just stared dumbly at the note and the hair. After a moment I wakened to the murmurs and jostling of people lined up waiting to pass by me to see the other displays. I moved out of the way and apologized, and quickly left the museum. When I got back to my apartment, I collapsed on the bed and fell into a state of oblivion that closely resembled unconsciousness.

I awoke sometime in the evening with a thunderous headache and no appetite for food. The house was quiet, though from time to time scattered voices and laughter reached me through the window overlooking the street. I pulled the chair over to the window and lit a cigarette. The air had cooled and there was a slight breeze, but I felt languid and dazed from the heat I had endured all day and from the alcohol that must still have been travelling through my veins. My whole body felt limp, as if my bones had melted, and it required all the energy I could summon to raise the cigarette to my lips. I closed my eyes and tried to empty my brain of thought. I succeeded, briefly, when an image of myself at the bus depot came into my head. There I was, checking the schedule, my packed bags beside me on the floor, my shoulders tense and my mind hostage to the countless anxieties brought on by enforced travel and an uncertain future.

I shook my head and gazed down at the street, my eyes following the movements of passersby. Finally, as the horizon dimmed and the air cooled further, Sonya emerged from the square into the cobbled lane, holding hands with Mischa and Peta. I shrank back from the window. In the midst of discussing something with her children she was smiling and laughing freely, and I suffered a momentary stab of guilt. Then my own problems loomed once more, obliterating everything else.

The clatter of feet on the stairs and steps in the hallway wrenched me out of another daydream, one in which I had boarded a train for an unknown destination. Then the door closed and all was quiet. I breathed in the air from the street. A few uneventful moments passed before an old man leading a donkey by a harness came along and directed the animal into a narrow passageway between two buildings. Seconds later some boys carrying wooden swords ran beneath my window. The echo of their shouts and laughter was still with me when the door across the hall creaked open. This was followed by the sound of tapping at my door.

I lit another cigarette. It was not the first time I had suffered this, the exquisite pain of exile, a pain that immobilizes the heart with longing even as it bleeds you of all desire to converse with others. It would pass in a day or two.

One of the conditions of my release was that I undergo regular psychiatric counselling. The case was assigned to a clinic, where I was to report twice a week for sessions that would last for at least two hours.

When I arrived for the first session I was surprised to find this sort of counselling taking place in a group setting. A young man, who seemed to be in charge, explained that trials had demonstrated it was beneficial for individuals who had suffered the effects of violence and those who had been the perpetrators of violent acts to come together in a place that was neutral and safe, and to speak openly about their experiences. He led me to a meeting room at the back of the clinic, where a dozen chairs had been arranged in a circle.

The group had been meeting regularly for months. Because membership was voluntary, people tended to come and go. I, however, had not been given a choice, and that evening, as the only new member, I was required to introduce myself to the others.

I told them my name and described where I was born and how I had come to be in this country. When nobody made any comment I went on to say that I was taking night classes and that I wanted to get a degree in psychology. After this I fell silent because I could think of nothing else that would interest them. I gazed around the circle. Every face was turned in my direction. They were male and female, young and old. One woman was pretty, another plain. I waited for them to ask me questions, but for some reason they seemed intimidated. Then the young man leading the group, whose name was Alex, asked me to tell everyone what I had done.

I said that after dating for a few weeks I had discovered that the woman I was in love with was having an affair with another man. I explained that where I came from this was considered the worst kind of insult. In tribal regions it was common for the man who was wronged to determine the punishment and dispense it at a time and place of his choosing. If he decided to kill the woman, he could do so in any way he liked, even in public if that's what he wanted. Since I lived in the city I had not seen anything like this when I was growing up, but I had been told of beheadings, floggings and mutilations. I had heard about a woman who had been chained to the back of a truck and dragged to her death along miles of dirt roads. People cheered as the truck went by, even other women. In another story a woman had been stripped and tied to a post in the main square of her village. Her husband had then invited people to express their disgust for her. All day she was pelted with rocks and smeared with excrement, and then, during the night, after the young men of the village had become drunk on the local wine, they took turns violating her. The next morning she was still alive, but her husband decided to leave her there because, as the saying goes, she had turned herself into garbage with her actions. No one gave her anything to eat or drink. Eventually she starved and her body was discarded in the forest. Officially the government prohibited these practices, but it was impossible to stamp out hundreds of years of tradition with a legislated package of reforms. As far as I knew, such atrocities continued to this day.

I didn't expect anyone in the group to applaud my actions, but I wanted them to know the context. After I found out that the woman I loved was having an affair I made plans to confront her. I don't know what I expected would happen, but I hoped that she would admit her guilt and promise never to see the other man again. I still loved her and wanted to believe she shared my feelings. We were to meet for dinner and when I went to her apartment I had my speech ready in my head. Her behaviour was the same as always, and when we kissed I could have sworn she was thinking of me and not someone else. We went to our favourite restaurant and over dinner I said that people I knew had seen her with this man. I told her I believed them and wanted her to stop seeing him. To my surprise she denied everything, even when I answered her denials with dates and times. She kept shaking her head. I was wrong, she said. These people I trusted were making a fool of me. I had had a few drinks before meeting her, and we were drinking wine with dinner. Soon I was very drunk. I tried to speak quietly, but my voice kept rising in my throat, and when I started to yell we were thrown out of the restaurant. She was disgusted with me by this time, but I was staggering drunk and I suppose she felt responsible, so she put me in a taxi and gave the driver my address.

I told the driver I wanted to go somewhere else. First we stopped at the liquor store, where I bought a bottle of whisky, and then I gave him the address of her apartment building. By the time we arrived I was calm, and I found it easy to pretend I was sober. I was lucky, because the doorman was helping an old woman down the steps and I slipped into the building without being seen. Going up in the elevator, I imagined that after putting me in the taxi she had called her lover. By now he was consoling her and caressing her and telling her to leave me, and this made me even angrier than I had been to start with. I didn't have a key to her apartment, so I waited in the stairwell and listened for movements in the corridor while I drank from the bottle. The building was always quiet and I knew that nobody had seen me. It wasn't long before she got home. I waited until she had inserted the key into the lock before approaching her. When she opened the door I gave her a push from behind. There was nothing she could do to defend herself. She flew forward, her head striking the wall as she went down. She was unconscious when she landed on the floor. I took a drink and looked at her. She seemed different to me now, like something soiled and rotten. I could hardly stand to touch her. I took her into the bedroom and laid her face down on the bed. I took her clothes off. Beneath her sweater and skirt she was wearing pink lingerie I had never seen before, and I guessed these were a gift from her lover. I went into the kitchen and found a dishtowel. I tore a strip from this and stuffed it into her mouth and used cellophane tape to bind and gag her. It was now after midnight and it occurred to me that she had not seen me come up to her from behind and would have no idea who was doing this to her when she awoke. I turned off all the lights and sat down.

I tipped the bottle of whisky up to my mouth. As the minutes went by my mind became crowded with images of the women I had heard about who had betrayed their husbands and who had suffered unspeakably as a result. These stories had been whispered in the schoolyard when I was young and recited at bars where I'd spent many of my evenings drinking before attaining legal age. I was always disgusted with the people who narrated these tales. I remembered laughter and raised glasses, but I thought it was nauseating, whether the stories were true or not, that civilized men could speak like this about the women they were supposed to love. When I considered these loutish companions of mine, I often thought it was no wonder their women looked elsewhere for kind words and gentle manners, tried to get away from ignorance and brutality and minds left dull from inactivity. Who could blame them for being dissatisfied with a role that would never allow them to be anything more than the bearers of children and playthings that their stupid husbands used to spend their lust?

After a while I fell asleep, but I woke up when the empty bottle rolled off my lap and clattered on the wooden floor. I opened my eyes and saw dimly that light was filtering into the room from outside. I realized that the sun was coming up and as my eyes regained a kind of focus and I saw where I was, the previous evening returned to me in all its horror. She was still on the bed, naked and lying on her stomach, her arms behind her bound together at the wrist, her legs bound at the ankle, and these bindings held together with more tape so that she could not move her arms or her legs. The gag was still in her mouth. As she struggled she made whimpering sounds that made me think of an animal caught in a trap. Then I giggled because what she suddenly reminded me of was a turkey trussed up and ready for the oven. I tried to stand up but reeled drunkenly. My stomach lurched with every move I made. As I unwrapped the tape from her arms and legs I fought against the pressure of vomit forcing its way up my throat. Her face was stained with tears. I pulled the gag from her mouth and heard my own voice telling her how sorry I was and asking her to forgive me. But I was laughing too, because the turkey image refused to go away. I couldn't stop laughing. My hands were shaking I was laughing so hard and I'm afraid I hurt her when I loosened the tape where it stuck to her skin. She didn't say a word. When she was free she jumped from the bed, grabbed the bottle, and struck me on the head. I fell to the floor, vomit spewing from my mouth. The last thing I remember before blacking out was the tremor in her voice as she spoke on the phone to the police.

As I talked I watched the other participants. Alex nodded and smiled encouragement whenever I paused or appeared unable to go on. The others seemed unsure how to respond. A few kept their eyes on me as I spoke, but some looked at the floor. As a group they seemed confused and embarrassed. I noticed in particular one older woman whose mouth was set in a prim scowl.

The next step in the process involved discussion of what I had told them, but nobody seemed willing to go first. After a few moments of unsuccessful prompting Alex got things started.

The discussion turned on my state of mind at the time of the assault. A woman asked if I'd ever imagined I could do something like that. Another remarked that culture was no excuse and that people made their choices according to their hearts. Then a young man in a jacket and tie asked if it had been raining on the night I had hurt my friend. I said I couldn't be certain, but it might have been. He explained that there are a lot of people who get depressed during bad weather, and that storms and rain showers can cause some people to lose control of their impulses. If you check the statistics, he argued, you'll see that the incidence of violence becomes more frequent as the weather worsens. There was scientific proof, he said. This provoked some harsh comments from others in the group and after a passionate exchange Alex intervened. During the pause in the discussion, someone asked me if I'd apologized to the woman I had terrorized. I said that I'd written her a letter to say I was sorry. But I hadn't actually seen her again because she refused to set foot in any room where I was present.

'No wonder,' the older woman said. 'You're an animal.'

I looked at her and tried to think of something to say, but before I could open my mouth, Alex told her that this sort of response was neither welcome nor helpful. To this she raised her chin and repeated what she'd said. Alex repeated what he'd said, but she refused to back down, and when he saw that arguing with her was pointless he moved the discussion on to other topics.

There was a girl sitting opposite me in the circle, and an hour later when the group broke up she was the only one who hadn't spoken. Her eyes were dark and her expression enigmatic. She had seemed to follow the discussion with interest, so I assumed she was just too shy to say anything in front of the group. I was about to approach her when Alex patted my arm and said he wanted to commend me for speaking truthfully and openly. It can be painful, he said, to recall the things we've done, especially when our remorse is genuine. But he was confident that the group would be more supportive when they got to know me better. I told him that, on the contrary, I didn't think the session had gone badly at all and I was looking forward to coming back. The others were talking among themselves now, and when Alex said goodbye I turned to where the girl had been, but she was gone.

I left the clinic and lit a cigarette as I walked. It was a clear night. I drew my gloves out of my pockets and pulled them on. When I'd left the bus shelter on the way here I'd noticed an all-night diner, and since it was cold and I was not in a hurry, I went in and took a seat in a booth. Someone had left behind that day's newspaper. A waitress came by and I ordered a cup of coffee. As I read about the events of the day, my mind returned to the therapy session. I suppose I could understand that having the perpetrators and victims of violence together in one room would force each to learn something about the other. But I didn't see how someone like me would benefit from this program. I was not a violent person and had only acted the way I had because of the alcohol. I wasn't looking for excuses, like the fellow who wanted to blame the weather. I knew I had hurt another person, but I preferred to think I would never do something like that again. The old woman seemed to think I was incorrigible, but I wanted her to know that my remorse was genuine, that I accepted my punishment and understood her disgust. I think more than anything I needed her to forgive me, and perhaps this was what Alex's program was all about.

The waitress brought my coffee and left, but I sensed someone else was standing nearby and when I looked up I saw the girl from the group session, the one who had not spoken. She was wearing a white winter coat with a fur-lined hood pulled back from her head.

'Do you mind if I sit down?' she asked. But she had already slid into the seat across from me. She smiled. She was very thin. Her neck was slender and her skin was so pale it hardly seemed real. Her gaze was unflinching and her eyes haunting in their loveliness.

'Do you want some coffee?' I asked. 'Or maybe something to eat?'

'Oh, no. I'm fine.'

She removed her gloves and shrugged off her coat. Settled now, she continued to smile. Beneath arched brows her eyes were a steely blue. She linked her hands together on the table.

'What is it?' I asked. Even though Alex had made the members of the group introduce themselves, I could not remember her name.

'What you did to that woman –'

I held up my hand.

'I'm not going to talk about it here,' I said.

She nodded and looked away.

'You did really well tonight. New people usually don't handle it as well as you.'

'How long have you been part of this group?'

'A year.' Then she seemed to think. 'Or maybe longer. I can't remember exactly.'

We were silent for a moment. When the waitress appeared and refilled my cup the girl smiled up at her.

'Is the process supposed to be humiliating?' I asked.

'Did you find it humiliating?'

'Not particularly. But I get the impression I'm supposed to feel chastened. I can't see any other reason for doing it. Actually, I don't feel anything.'

'Alex is a good man. He tries very hard.'

'I don't doubt his sincerity. But I'm not convinced that what he's doing is of value to the rest of us.'

She gazed at me as if she had nothing to hide, and I wondered if she had been a victim of violence, as I assumed the old woman had been. Or was she, like me, a perpetrator?

'You'll learn,' she said. 'It might take a while, but someday you'll see the worth in what he's doing.'

'A year is a long time,' I remarked after a moment when it seemed she had nothing more to say. 'Why is it taking you so long to get through this?'

She glanced down at the table. 'It's not easy to explain. There's something in me I'm learning to confront. I'm still not where I should be.'

All at once she seemed saddened or distressed. I waited for her to go on.

'What you did to that woman,' she said, 'you only did it because you loved her. I can see that. Love makes us do terrible things. But you only did what you had to. She should have been thankful. I think it's too bad she couldn't understand that you were telling her how much you loved her. If she had listened she would have heard what you were saying. But some people, you know, they never listen. Your friend didn't even try. I can tell she didn't from what you said. I only wish –' Here she attempted a smile, but instead the corners of her lips turned downward. 'It's what I've always wanted, someone who loves me enough to hurt me. You know. Really hurt me.'

I watched her. As the words tumbled from her mouth I caught them, one by one.

The night train to Shkodër was late. I waited on the platform for an hour, walking back and forth, smoking cigarette
after cigarette. There were about a dozen of us: a pale
young woman with a small boy asleep on her lap, some old people
wearing boots and heavy sweaters and carrying lumpish things in can-
vas bags, a man with a briefcase, an entire family – father, mother, and
three children – huddled on a bench. It was a cold night. The platform
was inside the station, but the end where the trains entered was open
to the weather. Then the announcement came: the train had broken
down and would not be repaired until morning.

I uttered a curse. Everyone else picked up their things and started
to leave. Apparently I was the only one who was agitated. The rest
filed out as if they'd expected this all along, as if waiting for a train that
was never going to come was part of the natural order of things.

Outside, I watched as my companions dispersed into the night. I
had not come prepared for cold. I zipped my jacket all the way up and
pulled the collar tight around my neck. There were no taxis, so I carried my bags the mile or so back to my hotel.

There was no longer a curfew, but since only a few lights were
working, the streets were quiet and dark. Once I'd left the train station behind, I saw no other pedestrians. Occasionally a car would
chug by with one or both headlights broken. Stray dogs roamed
through the remains of buildings damaged in the conflicts that had
occurred shortly after the Communists left power. Other than in the
main square, where the government offices and the university were
located, I had seen little evidence of rebuilding. It looked very much
the way I remembered it: a city suffering the effects of years of isola-
tion and neglect.

The same young man was behind the front desk when I got back.
I explained that the train had broken down and would not be running
until morning and asked if I could have my room for another night.

'No problem,' he said. Without looking at me, he slapped the key on the counter. He was smoking a cigarette and watching a soccer game on a tiny television. The reception was poor and he had to raise his voice above the static. 'But you will be fortunate if the train is running again in the morning.'

I had stepped away from the desk and returned when he spoke. 'Why is that?'

He shrugged.

'You're from here. You know what it's like. They have your money for the ticket. In the morning you'll go back to the train station and they'll tell you the train is out of service for good. Then someone will sell you another ticket for another train, and then that train will break down. The same with the third train. At least if you go to the bus station you can see there are buses and that they're running. You might even be able to get on one before it breaks down.'

I thought maybe he was joking and that he would smile when he saw that I understood. But he remained serious as he flicked ash from his cigarette and let it fall to the floor beneath the desk.

'Then how do people get around?'

He looked me up and down. Suddenly I was of more interest to him than the soccer game.

'Where are you trying to go?'

'Shkodër.'

He grabbed a piece of paper and scribbled something down.

'My nephew has a car. He will take you. It will cost fifty American dollars.'

'I paid twenty-five for my train ticket.'

He shrugged. 'When you buy another train ticket in the morning you'll have spent fifty dollars. And when that train breaks down, you'll be no closer to Shkodër than you are now. I'll be happy to help you when that happens. But tomorrow the price will be seventy-five.'

He stared at me and drew on the cigarette, his eyes set in an expression of lazy insolence. I knew he wanted my money, but he was good at pretending that he couldn't care less.

'I'll let you know in the morning what I want to do,' I said.

He shrugged. 'Do whatever you want. But remember that in the morning my nephew and his car might not be available. I could contact him now and tell him he's taking you to Shkodër tomorrow. That way he can prepare for the trip. But if I wait until morning he might have made other plans, or he might not feel like going. And the only way I can guarantee a rate of fifty dollars is if you give me the money in advance. That's how it works. Tomorrow it will be seventy-five. Tonight it is fifty. The decision is yours.'

He met my eyes briefly and then turned back to the soccer game.

Because of his manner I was tempted to take my chances at the train station in the morning. But I knew as well as he did that since the fall of the Communists not one train in the country had run on time. And the buses were worse, because they would take you halfway to your destination before breaking down and leaving you stranded. The books warned visitors that if they relied upon public transport they would probably be cheated. For example, none of the prices posted in the train or bus station had any bearing on the actual cost of the trip. The ride to Shkodër was supposed to cost thirteen dollars, but at the wicket the man took one look at me and seemed to decide to charge twenty-five. He told me the price on the sign had not been updated and that there were taxes, so I had no choice but to pay. We both knew what was going on and that he had just made himself twelve dollars richer. But since I wanted to reach my destination, I was forced into a game I had no wish to play. I paid what he asked, and when he gave me the ticket the receipt was for thirteen dollars.

'How do I know you even have a nephew?'

The clerk shrugged without looking at me. 'As I said, the decision is yours.'

The hotel lobby was dark and damp like a cave. It had a low ceiling and was dimly lit. Along the wall sat a couple of wobbly tables and some upholstered chairs that over long years of service had lost most of their stuffing along with their buoyancy. My ground-floor room had also seemed dank and unwholesome, an impression heightened by the fact that the window looked into a tangled overgrown garden sitting in an immobile pool of greenish water that would probably come alive with insects the moment the weather turned warm. I did not want to stay here another night, but it appeared I had no choice. I opened my wallet and took out fifty American dollars. I pushed the bills across the desk.

'When do you want to leave?'

'Early. Before seven.'

'He'll be waiting. His car is a red Zastava. It's old but good on mileage and it provides a comfortable ride. So don't worry. I won't be here, but if you bring your bags out front he'll see you.'

He folded the bills and slipped them into the pocket of his shirt.

'I can see you're skeptical,' he said with a laugh. 'Please, don't worry. This is not a trick. He'll be there. Go and have a good sleep. Believe me. Everything's taken care of.'

I nodded and lingered in the region of the desk for another minute. But since he didn't appear to be in a hurry to contact anyone I finally carried my bags down the hallway to my room. I tried not to think about how rashly I had parted with my money and where I had placed my trust. I would deal with whatever happened in the morning.

I awoke early, showered and dressed, and returned to the lobby with my packed bags. Someone had placed dishes of sliced sweet breads, butter, and a variety of sliced meats on one of the tables. On the other was a tall utensil for dispensing hot water, plastic cups, and powdered coffee, sugar and whitener. This was the complimentary breakfast I had been promised in the brochure. I did not take anything, because I recognized the bread and the meat as leftovers from the previous morning.

The sullen girl who had greeted me upon my arrival was seated at the desk. Her hair was lank and her skin bloodless, and she was wearing the same blue trousers and yellow T-shirt as the day before. Since they did not accept credit cards I gave her my key and paid my bill with cash. She refused to meet my eye and said nothing when I handed over the money, which she counted twice before issuing a receipt.

I went outside. It was November and should still have been warm, or at least temperate, but the wind coming from the north carried with it unwelcome hints of winter. The hotel was situated on a narrow lane several blocks from Skanderbeg Square, with its monuments and sporadic bursts of traffic and noise. It was, as a result, inexpensive and quiet, but also secluded and therefore dangerous if you were not careful. The police did not have a strong presence in the capital, and rival gangs now controlled different parts of the city. Muggings and assaults were common and police investigations rarely resulted in an arrest. Car theft was the crime of choice. In a country where the government had prohibited its citizens from owning a private vehicle as late as 1991, cars were in great demand, though few could afford to buy them. Half of the vehicles you saw on the street at any single time were stolen. The transition to democracy was progressing at a slow pace in my country, and in the meantime, while people struggled with the concept of representative government, the forces of anarchy seemed ever on the march.

I shivered as the wind buffeted the façade of the hotel and penetrated my thin jacket, the only outerwear I had brought. I had come back because I wanted to find out what had happened to my parents. After an absence of more than a decade it had not been easy for me to re-establish contact with friends from my past. But after sending out a great number of letters without receiving a single reply, I finally heard from a cousin on my mother's side, a young woman named Migena Morivic. She was living in Shkodër and attending the university there. Our correspondence, which began as a tentative process much like exploring unfamiliar terrain for invisible sinkholes, grew over two years into a regular and impassioned activity. My grandmother had been her great-aunt and our mothers had been cousins. I could remember a visit from her family when I was very young, but that was before she was born. And so, though we were related by blood and as far as we knew the only members of our family left alive, we had never met face to face. I had never heard her voice, nor she mine, because all of our attempts to reach each other by international telephone had failed. In the end, we had had to settle for an exchange of photographs.

I took the photograph from my wallet as I waited for my driver to appear. In it Migena stood at the corner of a stone building. A lengthy garbage-strewn boulevard stretched behind her, along the front of the building. The sky was the brilliant Adriatic blue I remembered so well. She was smiling and squinting into the camera, one hand raised to hold her hair away from her thin face. She had brown shoulder-length hair and appeared undernourished, for she was almost lost within her clothes, a sweater with sleeves so long they concealed all but the tips of her fingers, and ill-fitting denim jeans. Looking at her, it was difficult for me to believe that such a spindly, childlike creature could be in her twenties. But this was indeed the case. She had never mentioned a boyfriend, and I sometimes wondered, as I gazed into her eyes looking into the lens of the camera, who had taken the picture.

As our correspondence became more intimate, we exchanged stories of our families, and I told her the little I knew about my parents and their fate, which, because it was a mystery, invited speculation of the worst sort. I was very young at the time, no more than five or six, but memory has a way of seeping and accumulating and taking on the solidity of matter left undisturbed for many years, and I was not sure if what I related to her was fact, extravagant conjecture, or fiction. But without the least urging on my part, she had gone out and verified the essentials of the story I had given her.

She told me that in the province where I had lived with my parents there had been an influx of refugees fleeing conflicts taking place in other countries, and the military, recognizing that resources were scarce and fearing an uprising, conducted a general roundup of civilians and refugees. Our village, on Lake Scutari near Shkodër, was emptied of inhabitants. Most people were soon allowed to return to their homes, but others, for reasons that remain unclear, were held for longer periods, in some cases for up to a year. Because I was young I adapted easily to these new surroundings and almost forgot what it was like to live in a house. The temporary school was a single room constructed of rough wooden planks, and I attended every day with the other children who were confined to the camp.

It was on a day that had nothing special about it that a woman came to the school to meet me after class had ended. Normally my mother came for me and we walked together to our tent, which we shared with another family. But instead, the woman led me to a bus, where some other children were already waiting. She said we were going on an adventure and that our parents had given permission. We were driven into the city and I was placed in an orphanage. I never returned home and I never saw my parents again. When stories of ethnic cleansing and mass graves began to surface a few years ago, I made inquiries of the interior ministry but was always told the information was classified. Then my cousin Migena told me she had found someone who was willing to talk, and I decided I could no longer postpone the trip home.

I was surprised when a red Zastava, dappled with rust, appeared at the end of the lane and drew up in front of the hotel, for I was convinced I had been cheated and that I would soon be making my way to either the bus depot or the train station. A slight young man wearing a soiled linen shirt, jeans and leather shoes climbed out. His hair was cut very short and his skin had a swarthy Mediterranean cast to it.

'I am sorry to have kept you waiting,' he said. 'I am Ahmet.' We shook hands and he lifted my bags before I could do it myself.

'Please, it's no problem for me. You are going to Shkodër?'

'Yes.'

He opened the trunk of the car and tossed the bags in.

'Then we must move quickly. It's a long drive and the roads are bad, and there will be rain, which could make it difficult.'

'Don't you find it cold?' I asked as we got in the car.

He laughed and I noticed a gap where one of his front teeth was missing. 'You see what I am wearing? When these are worn out I will have to buy more. In the meantime …' He shrugged and laughed again.

He manoeuvred the stick shift and the car lurched forward.

'We will have to buy gas,' he said after a moment. 'You will pay?'

I looked at him.

'My uncle did not mention this.' He shook his head. 'I will have to tell him, you know, this is not fair. People should be warned.' He motioned with his hand as he drove. 'But it's okay. We will share the cost since you didn't know.'

'I don't mind,' I said. 'I should have enough for gas. But I'll have to go to a bank when we get to Shkodër.'

The car rattled through a pothole as we turned the corner on to the Boulevard of the Martyr of the Nation. We passed the soccer stadium and were soon approaching Skanderbeg Square. Along here were buildings constructed by the Italians during the war. They were now filled with government offices and they shone with fresh paint. There was not a scrap of garbage. The statue of Georg Kastrioti Skanderbeg on his stallion gleamed as if recently polished. Hundreds of years ago he had defended the Christian citizens of our outpost nation against the Turks, and was now immortalized for his heroism and his sacrifice. Next to the statue were the mosque and the clock tower, and, nearby, the Palace of Culture and the National Museum. A few adventurous tourists milled about. The cafés were just opening.

'And what is awaiting you in Shkodër?' Ahmet asked as he veered the car off to the right and up an unmarked side street. 'You don't have to tell me if you don't want to. But it is a long time to go without talking of something.'

'I'm visiting a relative.'

'Ah,' he said. 'So do you have a lot of relatives up north?'

'Just one, I'm afraid,' I said. 'A cousin. We've never met.'

He nodded. 'Where do you live?'

'I've been living abroad.'

He glanced over at me. 'Can I ask where?'

'Greece for a while,' I said. 'But I was lucky enough to find a sponsor who helped me get a job in America.'

Ahmet whistled through the gap between his teeth.

'So, you are making good money.' He smiled and rubbed two fingers against his thumb. 'American dollars.'

'I've been studying,' I said. 'I've also done some teaching, but only for short periods. What I want to do is teach full time.'

'You have your own apartment?'

'Yes,' I said. 'A small one.'

'Cable TV? A hundred channels?'

'I don't own a television. It's a waste of time.'

Ahmet nodded in thoughtful fashion. 'The women are friendly?' he asked. When I hesitated he added, 'We hear stories, you know. American women. They will spend all your money and then leave you to pay their debts.'

'I think,' I said, 'the women in America are the same as everywhere else.'

Ahmet opened his mouth and laughed as if I'd made a joke. I watched the gap move up and down.

'Is it good there?'

He cast me a sly glance.

'I mean, do they welcome you? Because, you know, we hear things about how they treat foreigners in America. Every day people are beaten and put in jail for no reason. If you are different, or if you have dark skin, it is sometimes not so good.'

'I've always been treated well,' I said. 'I don't know who's telling you this, but they're wrong.'

Ahmet nodded. We were passing through a partly ruined neighbourhood on the outskirts of the city. The buildings were full of mortar holes and the street was nothing but a strip of packed dirt. The car rattled and wheezed each time we encountered a bump or a pothole. Ahmet did not slow down, even when there were people or pigs or goats crossing our path. He veered around these and other obstacles with the graceful precision of someone who has been driving for a long time, even though he did not appear to be any older than my cousin Migena.

We stopped for gas at a station with a single pump, where Ahmet was only too glad to let me cover the cost of filling the tank. Soon we were driving along a narrow winding highway, heading into the mountainous north. As we rose into the hills, the forest on either side of the highway grew thick with the native broad-limbed pine. The tarmac was old, pitted, strewn with loose stone. There was no dividing line. The sky was overcast and a few drops of rain hit the windshield. In the distance, to our left, was the sea. From time to time a vehicle whizzed by heading south. I shifted my position in the seat, trying to make myself comfortable, but the old Zastava did not offer much leg room.

Every few minutes I noticed Ahmet looking at me and smiling. 'What is it?' I asked.

He shook his head as if amazed. 'America,' he said with a wide grin, showing me the gap where his front tooth had been.

It was late afternoon when we made our descent from the highlands toward Shkodër and I saw, for the first time in more than a decade, Rozafa Castle huddled in the distance. The poor condition of the roads had held us up. Whole sections had been washed away in the spring storms and not repaired. Our progress had also been slowed by horse-drawn carts that crawled down the middle of the highway and were impossible to pass for miles at a time. Fortunately, the rain that had seemed imminent as we began our journey had never materialized. As Ahmet let me out in front of the National Bank, the sun emerged from behind some clouds and I felt its warmth for the first time since my arrival.

I went inside and made a withdrawal from my account, a procedure that required the completion of several lengthy forms, a phone call, and the signatures of at least five people. At each step in the transaction the young female clerk watched me sign my name with the unsmiling fixity of someone who suspects underhanded dealings are in progress and is determined not to be cheated. Finally, without a word, as if grudgingly performing a kindness for someone who has no right to expect such favours, she gave me my money.

Ahmet was leaning on the car examining his fingernails when I came out.

'It's too late to start driving home now,' he explained when I questioned him. 'I can take you where you want to go.' He shrugged. 'If that's convenient.'

'Where will you stay?'

'I have friends,' he said. 'And if they are not home I'll sleep in the car. It wouldn't be the first time.'

I was reluctant to part with more of my cash, especially as it had been obtained with such difficulty. But I was warming to him. I opened the door and got in.

'Would you like to meet my cousin?'

We drove toward the university. Migena lived in a dormitory, sharing a room with another student, whose name, I recalled from one of her letters, was Erika. We still had not spoken. I had tried to phone her from the hotel, but the connection had not gone through. However, she was expecting me. My last letter had contained details of my travel arrangements, and she had written back to tell me that she had noted the date of my arrival and would be there to greet me.

Shkodër is an old town that has made an uneasy transition into a small city. Its history goes back to Roman times, but because geography places it at a natural crossroads it has always been a cultural centre, an easy target for invaders, and a catalyst for political transformation, even during the darkest days of the Communist stranglehold. It was here that the democracy movement gained both legitimacy and momentum. Students gathered in the street demanding the end of one-party rule. Many were arrested and some were killed, but a movement that began with a group of ragged young people waving placards and chanting slogans spread through the country and eventually brought down a regime that had held power for nearly half a century.

We passed new buildings and old houses, lined up beside each other along narrow streets; awkward neighbours. Here, as elsewhere, there was garbage strewn about and hunched figures in rags seeking alms, but I had seen so much of this since arriving I hardly noticed it any more. The university, a collection of ugly brick and concrete structures in poor repair, squatted in the middle of the modern downtown, close by the Pedagogical Institute, with which it was not affiliated. There were few directional signs and none of those we saw made mention of a student residence. To avoid driving in circles I told Ahmet to park the car. We got out and asked a young man which way to go.

The door of the residence stood wide open. A uniformed man at a desk merely glanced at us when we entered. By now the sun had edged toward the horizon and the air had grown chill. Ahmet in his thin clothes seemed glad to be indoors.

I found Migena's room and knocked on the door. When she answered I experienced a shock of recognition and felt my emotions veer out of control. Tears filled my eyes. She cried my name aloud and in an instant we were in each other's arms. In my mind I saw the photograph and thought how strange it was that this could be the same person, for the girl in the picture had been without substance for so long it was almost as if my imagination had conjured her out of air and wishful thoughts. But she was real, and as we hugged I realized that people can suffer the pain of being apart from one another even though they have never met. In my travels I had known many people; some had even become my friends. But who among them had accepted me in that first moment, without question, without reservation? The feeling that came over me as Migena said my name and clutched me around the neck was something I had never known until that day, the certainty that I was home.

Her body seemed mostly bones and I loosened my embrace for fear of harming her.

'I thought you had changed your mind and weren't coming,' she said as we separated. 'I was expecting you this morning.'

'The train broke down. I got a drive. This is my friend Ahmet.'

Ahmet stepped forward and nodded stiffly. There was an awkward pause as neither spoke and Migena's eyes narrowed. Ahmet looked toward the floor.

'I'll leave you now,' he said, backing away. 'Good luck with the rest of your journey.'

'You have a car?'

Migena's tone had shifted to become formal, businesslike.

'Yes.'

She turned to me. 'Can he be trusted?'

'What's going to happen that we have to worry about people being trustworthy?'

We were standing in the open doorway to her room. After a few seconds she seemed to reach a decision.

'Come in,' she said, addressing both of us.

Migena explained that through a friend she had made contact with someone in the interior ministry and learned that excavation of a mass grave was underway about fifty miles to the north. Camps, like the one I remembered, where my parents and I were taken, had been located in the area. Records still existed that proved this, but even though the government officially denied knowledge of these camps, unofficially they were willing to make concessions to those whose lives had been altered by the insane brutality of the previous regime.

The only problem, she said, had been transportation. But if Ahmet could take us in his car . . .

She had been told that unofficial permission had been granted for us to visit the excavation site, where the items that had been found were being sorted and, if possible, identified. I would be free to look over the personal items so far uncovered. If anything that had belonged to my parents was among them, I would have my answer.

'It's not like you are going there to find justice,' she said, her voice making me think of someone giving instructions to a small child. 'But if you don't go you will have lost an opportunity to find out what happened.'

'And if there's nothing?'

'If you find nothing,' Ahmet said, 'then you are no worse off than you were before.'

Migena looked at him. To this point he had sat apart from us in silence as he seemed with difficulty to absorb the story behind why I had come here.

'That's the way it looks to me,' he said in answer to her scrutiny. He shrugged and looked away.

Migena's expression remained serious. 'He's right. There's no reason not to go.'

'Except that when we find nothing I won't know where to go next.'

'There are other burial sites,' Migena said. 'Dozens at last count. If necessary we'll petition to visit these as well.'

I nodded. 'Why the need for secrecy?'

'Well, as you can imagine, none of this is common knowledge. If you can believe it, there is still a faction of communists operating in the area. If they knew about the excavations it is possible they might do something to prevent them. They're dangerous, to put it simply. Disorganized but dangerous. Every now and then you see a poster stuck to a wall saying what a wonderful man Hoxha was and that the stories about him ordering the murder of villagers who resisted his policies and selling prehistoric artefacts on the black market so he could enlarge his house are lies. The police take the posters down. But, still, you never know who might sympathize. You have to be careful. Your friend here,' she said, indicating Ahmet. 'He might be a Communist who will take all of this and report back to his comrades.'

Ahmet laughed out loud, once again showing us the gap between his front teeth. 'What? You really think this? Are you crazy?'

'No,' I said, looking at Migena. 'She doesn't think this.'

It was getting late and none of us had eaten. Migena's room provided only basic comforts: two beds, two desks, some chairs, shelves with books. She had no place to keep food and took all her meals in the cafeteria.

'Where is Erika?' I asked. I had just noticed this obvious absence.

'She has a boyfriend and stays with him on the weekends. I like it because it gives me privacy and I can get some work done.'

'You don't have a boyfriend?' Ahmet asked.

Migena laughed. 'Who has time for that? I'm too busy as it is. After class I have assignments and I volunteer with the student newspaper.'

'You should have a boyfriend,' Ahmet said with some force. Migena turned and for a moment they stared at each other.

I stood and suggested we all go somewhere to eat, and then Ahmet and I could make arrangements for the night.

We left the residence and walked quickly because of the cold. Migena led us a short distance along the main street to a restaurant that even at this hour was crowded with students and noisy with their talk. The tables and chairs were made of white moulded plastic, like lawn furniture, and when we received our food, it was served on cardboard plates. Migena spoke to the friends she met and introduced me as her cousin 'from America'. I had planned to bring up the subject of her emigrating as well, but she seemed very happy here, among people she knew and who knew her, so I held this back. As we ate, she spoke in general terms about life in Shkodër, about exploring the forest around Rozafa Castle, the refugee problem, the corruption and ineptitude of the government. She had told me in a letter that she planned to pursue advanced study in archaeology, and I asked her about that. She held an opinion on every subject that came up, from American foreign policy to the clear-cutting of the Brazilian rainforest to Ismail Kadare's chances of winning the Nobel Prize. It seemed as if each topic of discussion was the one weighing most heavily upon her mind at that moment. Ahmet said little but did not take his eyes from her. Whenever there was a pause in the conversation he questioned her, and after a while it was obvious he was doing this just to keep her talking.

It was after ten when we left the restaurant. In the two hours we had spent eating and talking the temperature had dropped further. None of us was dressed for it and we sprinted back to the residence building.

'Don't worry about trying to find a hotel tonight,' Migena said, drawing a laboured breath as we went inside and closed the door behind us. 'You can both stay in my room.'

'Where will you sleep?' I asked.

'One of the girls down the hall has a room with two beds but no roommate. I'll stay with her.'

Ahmet and I looked at each other and then at her.

'It's really no problem.' She smiled and touched my arm.

Migena showed us where the toilets were, retrieved some things from her room, and left us. Within minutes Ahmet was asleep in Erika's bed. He had kicked off his shoes but had not taken the time to undress. His limbs were long and his thin body angular. He lay sprawled on the bed like a corpse.

I looked at his shoes. They were old black leather loafers, likely manufactured in Bulgaria. The leather was creased and soft from constant wear, and the soles of both were worn through. He had no socks. I thought sadly of his feet, exposed to the elements with each step. We had spoken a great deal during the drive to Shkodër. His two older brothers had died, one many years ago of tuberculosis and the other in a clash with police. His parents occupied a small apartment and had lost their savings in an investment scam. He supported them by operating a small taxi service, but wanted a better life for the children he would have later on. I tried to sound encouraging when I said that his business venture would succeed. He was ambitious and not lacking in intelligence, but there was every chance the life awaiting him would be short and filled with hardship.

Gradually his breathing slowed and settled into a rhythm. I had noticed his attraction to Migena. But I could not allow them to become involved. I would find an opportunity to speak to her about coming to America to study. I would help her become a citizen of that great land. I would introduce her to my friends and see that she had everything she wanted. Until now I had lived a selfish life. That was going to change.

There were sounds coming from outside. I drew back the curtain. Snow was falling. It was after midnight. People were running about in the circle of light thrown by a street lamp, drawn out of doors by the snow. I had heard their laughter. They gathered the snow in their bare hands and threw it. They chased each other, moving in and out of the circle of light, disappearing into the darkness, and then returning. A few others joined them. I thought then of what I was going to do tomorrow, and I wondered if the mass grave we were to visit in the morning actually held my parents' remains. Would I recognize my father's watch, my mother's ring, if I were to come across them? What if they had been robbed before being killed? Would anything remain of them? How would it feel, to know that your parents had been forced by armed men to march into the hills and then shot in the back of the head? How would it feel, to know you had been spared the same fate simply because it was a school day? How could anyone hope to understand a world in which such a thing could happen?

The snow came down, and I imagined it falling on the grave of my parents, covering it. I wished we were not going to that place in the morning, but I would go. I would tell Migena, yes, this is my father's watch, this is my mother's ring. And I would carry them to her and place them in her hand.

Acknowledgements

Five of the stories in this volume were published previously: 'Pirgi' in *The Antigonish Review* #141/42; 'Night Train' in *Grain* 33/1; 'Evidence' ('The plane went down …') in the anthology *Transits* (Invisible Publishing); 'The Cure' ('One of the conditions of my release …') in *Front & Centre* #16; 'Proof' (The first thing I saw when I awoke …') in *ATLAS: New Writing, Art & Image* #2.

*

While writing these pieces I saw no need to strive for geographical or historical accuracy. Places and events mentioned in these pages may bear a resemblance to actual places and events, but they are only props employed to make the narrative more vivid than it might otherwise have been.

Thanks

Every book is a collaborative project. This one owes its existence to many people.

Richard Cumyn read an early draft of these stories, spotted a great many errors and infelicities of language, and made numerous recommendations that have been incorporated into the text. His input has been invaluable and his friendship priceless. Deborah-Anne Tunney confirmed that the early version was worth the time and effort it would require to make it better. Her continuing support has been a luxury in good times and a crutch in bad.

Doris Cowan's dexterous editing and uncompromising standards have given the text its present form. To her I am deeply indebted. Any errors that may have wriggled through her editorial net are the sole responsibility of the author.

I want to thank members of the Nova Scotia writing community for their encouragement over the years, especially when the prospect of publication seemed remote: Brian Bartlett, Andy Wainwright, Malcolm Ross, Karen Smythe, Sue MacLeod, Susan Kerslake, Jeanette Lynes, Lesley Choyce. At the Writers' Federation of Nova Scotia, Jane Buss has tirelessly advocated on behalf of writers for more than a decade. Her superhuman efforts have made it possible for many of us toiling in obscurity to finally say, 'I am a writer.'

I want to acknowledge the generous support of the Canada Council for the Arts.

It was in 1998 at the Hawthornden Castle International Retreat for Writers in Lasswade, Scotland, that some of these pieces took very early form. I want to thank the judges who deemed me worthy of a Hawthornden Fellowship and especially Adam Czerniawski, administrator during my stay, for unparalleled hospitality and a quiet corner in which to indulge my craft.

I wish to thank colleagues and staff at Dalhousie University's Killam Library for twenty years of forbearance and encouragement.

At the Humber School for Writers Summer Workshops of 2002, 2003 and 2004, I was fortunate to work with Isabel Huggan, Alistair MacLeod, and Wayson Choy, who, on a personal and professional level, offered mentorship and camaraderie. I value their wisdom, insight, and guidance. In 2005 on the last day of the Tin House Summer Writers Workshop, Dorothy Allison said to me, 'You'll be all right.' I wasn't as confident as she was.

Steven Heighton and Mary Jo Anderson championed my writing to others and provided advice and friendship when it counted most.

Thanks to Gordon MacDonald for permission to use his painting *Leaving Saint John* as the cover image.

My parents never doubted that someday all that scribbling would result in a published book.

Most importantly, my wife Collette endured the years of rejection and self-doubt by my side and never wavered in her conviction that my efforts were worthwhile. Her love and friendship carried me through the tough times. I am privileged to be able to share my life and modest successes with her.

Ian Colford's first story was published in 1983 and he has subsequently had fiction, reviews and essays published in a variety of periodicals. Travel to Greece, Portugal, Turkey and Italy have laid a foundation upon which much of his recent fiction is constructed. His work has won awards and has been short-listed for the Journey Prize. He lives in Halifax and for the last twenty years has laboured at Dalhousie University. *Evidence* is his first collection.